THE REPUBLIC OF TRŮPIS

HAÏLJI
THE REPUBLIC OF UŽUPIS

DALKEY ARCHIVE PRESS
Champaign / London / Dublin

Originally published in Korean as *Ujup'isŭ Konghwaguk*
by Minumsa, Seoul, 2009

Copyright ©2009, Haïlji
Translation copyright ©2013, Bruce and Ju-Chan Fulton
Poems on p.95 and pp.128–132 written in English by Haïlji

First edition, 2014
All rights reserved

Library of Congress Cataloging-in-Publication Data
Ha, Il-chi, 1955-
  [Ujup'isu Konghwaguk. English]
  The Republic of Uzupis / Haolji ; translated from the Korean
by Bruce and Ju-Chan Fulton. -- First edition.
     pages cm
  ISBN 978-1-62897-065-4 (pbk. : alk. paper)
  I. Fulton, Bruce, translator. II. Fulton, Ju-Chan, translator. III. Title.
  PL992.24.I43U5813 2014
  895.73'5--dc23
                                           2014016361

Library of Korean Literature

Partially funded by the Illinois Arts Council, a state agency
Published in collaboration with the Literature Translation
Institute of Korea

www.dalkeyarchive.com

Cover: design and composition by Mikhail Iliatov
Printed on permanent/durable acid-free paper

CONTENTS

9 | CHAPTER 1 Jonas the Taxi Driver

17 | CHAPTER 2 The People of Hotel Užupis

26 | CHAPTER 3 Chez Eigis

37 | CHAPTER 4 Vladimir of the Silver Hair

46 | CHAPTER 5 Nocturnal Encounters

54 | CHAPTER 6 Tomas, Prime Minister of Užupis

65 | CHAPTER 7 For the Love of Vilma

75 | CHAPTER 8 At Café Mano

85 | CHAPTER 9 Jurgita's Husband

98 | CHAPTER 10 Poets of a Colonized Land

108 | CHAPTER 11 Marija, the Flower Girl

117 | CHAPTER 12 The Swallows in the Drawers

126 | CHAPTER 13 Jurgita of Adutiskis

138 | CHAPTER 14 Down by the Vilnia River

THE REPUBLIC OF UŽUPIS

CHAPTER 1 Jonas the Taxi Driver

When the Asian man appeared at immigration control, the official, a young woman in an olive-green uniform, was startled. Asians were not a common sight in this country. With an amiable smile the man presented his passport. As the woman flipped through it, her face took on a solicitous expression. She spoke briskly into a telephone, a note of urgency in her voice. Then she turned back to the man.

"Mr. Hal, someone will be with you shortly."

And soon two other officials arrived, border control agents. They were dressed like the woman and they were armed. One of the men was gigantic, six and a half feet tall. The first thing they did was size up this man Hal, a clean-shaven, neatly dressed gentleman in his early forties. He was calm and thoughtful, his demeanor refined.

"Your boarding pass, please," said the big agent.

What to make of this request? Granted, the big man's accented English was a challenge, but who expects to be asked for a boarding pass at the immigration booth? Besides, the other arrivals were proceeding through immigration without a hitch. Why was Hal being singled out—it didn't make sense.

"Boarding pass," said the other agent, also in English, extending his hand. "Boarding pass!"

When Hal finally responded his voice was polite but firm. He had presented his boarding pass at the departure gate in Amsterdam, why were they demanding it from him now that he had arrived? He didn't understand.

The two agents were taken aback. Was their command of English so weak that they could not understood Hal?

The young woman stepped in: "You are 'no visa,'" she explained to Hal, "which means your stay in this country is limited to fifteen days. But before we can admit you, we need proof that you will leave the country within that time. That's why we're asking for your return ticket to Amsterdam."

Hal shrugged. "But I'm not returning to Amsterdam, my destination is elsewhere, and I didn't purchase a round-trip ticket. You're not saying you're denying me entry because I don't have a round-trip ticket, are you?"

The young woman interpreted for the two agents, who conferred with each other, their expressions grave, before giving the woman some instructions.

The woman turned back to Hal: "When do you plan to leave the country?"

"As soon as I can. By the end of the day, if possible."

The woman was dubious as she interpreted for the agents. The two men instructed the woman further.

"And where is your final destination?"

"The Republic of Užupis."

When this response was relayed to them, the two agents conferred once again, this time at some length, and came to a decision. After issuing one last directive to the woman they left.

The young woman produced a form and asked Hal to sign it, and when this was done she stamped his passport. "We are admitting you for forty-eight hours. If you are unable to exit the country in that time, it is your responsibility to report to the office at the Ministry of Foreign Affairs that deals with foreign nationals; there is the address." And the woman returned Hal's passport along with the form.

Hal thanked her and was proceeding past the booth when she asked him one last question.

"The Republic of Užupis?"

"That's right."

"Where is *that*?"

Why would she ask such a question? Hal didn't answer.

Having changed some money, Hal left the terminal, overcoat draped over his arm. It was snowing and there was a sodden chill in the air. Hal donned the coat. It was stylish and of an excellent weave but too lightweight for the severe winters of this land.

Outside the terminal was a sleepy, nondescript plaza. It reminded Hal of a train station you might find in a small city in the countryside. A file of yellow taxis, a dozen or so, awaited fares, and a short distance off, a blue metro bus sat idling; there were no other vehicles. The plaza had turned into a sheet of ice, and beyond it spread a grove of birches. Hal didn't know what to make of it all—he had never seen such a small, unprepossessing international airport.

"Where to, sir?"

One of the taxi drivers snagged Hal, a man whose hair had turned white, but who couldn't have been older than his mid-forties. His English was passable.

"Užupis," said Hal.

"Užupis?" said the driver, as if he had never heard the name before.

"Yes, the Republic of Užupis."

"Republic?" The man looked even more puzzled.

Hal produced a postcard and offered it to the driver. "Here's the address. I think maybe it's not so far from here. It's postmarked Vilnius, Lithuania."

The man put on reading glasses and inspected the postcard, then approached his fellow drivers, who were huddled nearby, and asked them what they made of it. Stamping their cold feet, the drivers looked at the postcard and debated with one another, occasionally glancing in Hal's direction. Finally Hal set down his suitcase on the ice-covered plaza. Turning up the collar of his coat and putting on a pair of gloves, he took in his surroundings.

Shrouded by the falling snow and the advancing dusk, the birches at the far end of the plaza seemed to be floating on air. The blue bus admitted one last passenger and set off toward the birches—beyond which the city must have been located—and before long it too was floating through the falling snow. The plaza lapsed into desolate silence.

And then an imploring voice cried out: "Jurgita!"

Startled, Hal turned to see a beautiful young blonde with a doleful expression. Floundering toward her was a bulky, middle-aged man, a farmer by the look of him, clutching to his chest a huge goose. It was he who had called out the soulful "Jurgita!" presumably the name of the beautiful young maiden. The melodramatic meeting of this graceful woman and the comical farmer was like something out of a play. Impervious to it all, the snow continued to fall.

"Okay, let's go!"

The driver was back. He returned the postcard, and while he loaded Hal's suitcase into the trunk Hal continued to gaze at the encounter between Jurgita and the farmer. Whereas the farmer was overcome with emotion and about to burst into tears, Jurgita remained still, her expression as doleful as before. She could have been a princess returning home from a long exile, being welcomed by a former servant whose station had fallen to that of a rustic.

"Please," said the driver, gesturing toward the back seat. With one last look at Jurgita, Hal climbed in.

The taxi was a vintage make and apparently finicky in cold weather, for it was reluctant to start. After turning the engine over several times in vain, the driver opened the door, planted his left foot on the icy road, and managed to rock the vehicle several yards forward, at which point he released the clutch and the engine finally engaged. Back in went the driver's foot, the door shut, and off they went.

The first scene they passed was that of the other taxi drivers, big, well-built men stamping their feet, shoulders hunched up against the cold. They gazed vacantly at Hal as the taxi went past.

The next image was that of Jurgita and the farmer. Jurgita still looked doleful and she still hadn't moved. Depositing the goose on the icy ground, the farmer hefted her bags. Hal looked back at the retreating scene, drawn by the intensity of Jurgita's beauty. She might have been looking his way, but he couldn't be sure. Presently she was out of sight.

The taxi continued toward the birches, and as they passed the grove the driver turned on the radio and Hal heard a broadcast that he assumed to be in Lithuanian, not a word of which he understood. He wondered if it was the news.

Beyond the birches, Hal saw the outline of the city. Gray buildings came into view, dreary structures that might have been factories or apartments. He felt no warmth from this scenery, though these buildings too, owing to the fall of the snow and the night, seemed to be floating in the distance. And yet he felt buoyant as he gazed out the window, anticipating his imminent arrival at his destination.

Some ten minutes later the taxi suddenly braked and turned onto a through street. There wasn't much traffic and the snow had accumulated on the road, which was flanked by barren, snow-covered lots, beyond which rose somber, grimy apartment buildings.

Hal watched, uncomprehending, as the taxi went in this new direction. The driver too, so sure of himself when they had left the airport, looked left and right, examining each sign they passed—had he lost his way? The strange thing was, the road itself was not difficult to follow, not the sort of road where a person might get lost.

Finally, on a deserted stretch on the outskirts of the city, the driver came to a stop. "Would you please show me that address once more?"

Hal handed the postcard to the man, who once again put on his glasses to examine it. Then he pocketed the glasses and proceeded to slowly cruise along, examining each road sign as if expecting Hal's destination to appear. Hal was disbelieving: Did the driver really think he was going to find the Republic of Užupis on the outskirts of this dismal city? And all the while the meter was running.

The driver pulled over and stopped again, set the hand brake, and got out. "I'll be right back." And off he went through the snow across a vacant lot toward an aging apartment building in the distance. Hal couldn't help thinking the man had decided to milk his foreign passenger for all he was worth.

The driver approached three people standing outside the building and spoke to them. Inside the taxi Hal smirked: *Let's see how much you try to squeeze me for.* The unintelligible broadcast still issued from the radio and the meter still was clicking, the fare working its way up. Above the meter was a clock that read 4:47. Hal removed his watch and re-set the time. And then he found himself coughing. How damp and chilly it was inside the old taxi! So much for the heater.

Just then Hal noticed a hefty, middle-aged man plodding through the snow. Balanced across his shoulders was a massive grandfather clock. His clothing was shabby and he appeared exhausted—he must have toted his heavy burden a long distance. It was a curious sight, the man's leaden steps dislodging snow and the clock that rested on his shoulders looking rather like a coffin. Hal watched, fascinated.

As the driver made his way back to Hal, he and the man with the clock crossed paths. But neither man seemed aware of the other. Each walked on in silence.

"I'm sorry," said the driver once he was back inside. But just as they were pulling away, a taxi approached from the opposite direction. Hal's driver quickly brought his vehicle to a halt, set the brake, rolled down the window, and beckoned the other driver. The second taxi came up close. Down came the driver's window and out popped the head of a man who looked very young for a taxi driver. The two drivers began a conversation, unintelligible to Hal. Hal's driver handed the postcard to the other man, who inspected it and then, looking exasperated, got out of his taxi. Hal's driver got out as well, and the two men continued their conversation, at one point the younger man fishing out a cell phone and punching in a number. The fare kept climbing. When would the conversation end? Waiting patiently, Hal was hit with a wave of drowsiness and began to nod off. He heaved a yawn and shook his head to clear it. Jet lag was setting in.

"Okay," said Hal's driver when he finally returned. The sky was distinctly darker.

"All right, you've had your fun, yes?" said Hal, who had finally lost patience. "The game's over—let's be on our way."

The driver's embarrassment was almost palpable. But he didn't respond—perhaps he hadn't understood? Instead he swung the taxi about and set off in the direction from which they had come. The bleak scenery passed by in reverse. Hal watched the still unfamiliar landscape, but with no interest. Night was falling .

They drove through the twilight, stopping at a railroad crossing while a dark, interminably long freight train passed. Hal fell asleep.

When he lurched awake, there was light outside. How far had they come? Hal saw a city street, but it was lifeless, snow accumulating all about.

The taxi made a circle on the plaza in front of an antiquated white building. Where were they? Hal asked. City Hall, replied the driver in a gruff tone. He must have been upset that he wouldn't be able to string Hal along any further.

They left the plaza, turned down a dark, narrow alley, and crossed a bridge. Hal noticed a sign—"Airport 6 km." So, an hour to travel six kilometers.

Across the bridge the taxi came to a stop. Finally. The driver got out and opened the trunk to retrieve Hal's suitcase.

Hal climbed out and saw, faintly lit by a streetlight, a forlorn side street. At the foot of the light pole the snow continued to accumulate.

"That will be eighty-five *litas*," said the driver after he had set down Hal's suitcase. "But let's say sixty, because I was a little lost back there."

Hal looked about in a daze.

"Don't get me wrong," said the driver. "I'm actually a professor. I only do this on the side—that's why I don't know the roads so well."

The part about not knowing the roads was presumably a bald-faced lie, but there seemed to be an element of truth to the claim that he was a professor: not many cab drivers could be expected to have such a good command of English.

"But this isn't Užupis," said Hal in a restrained voice.

"No, this is the right place—no doubt about it," said the driver as he indicated a dilapidated three-story building. On the front of the building a small neon sign reading Hotel Užupis blinked on and off.

Hal clapped a hand to his forehead in dismay. "I said Republic of Užupis, not Hotel Užupis!"

The driver became agitated; he was in a fix.

"Well, no matter," said Hal as he produced a hundred-*litas* note from his wallet and offered it to the driver. "It's dark already—I guess it'll be all right if I spend the night in this hotel and go the rest of the way tomorrow."

The driver relaxed. He reached into his pocket for change.

Hal made a dismissive gesture. "Forget it. Consider it a tip—nice job with that little game you played."

The driver was skeptical. But when he finally realized Hal was in earnest, he became ecstatic: "Oh, thank you, thank you! You are so generous, sir! A true gentleman, sir!" And then he bowed.

Hal was disgusted.

"I tell you what," said the driver. "If you wish to go to the Republic of Užupis, then I will be your guide—I will take you there tomorrow. You see, I have no classes tomorrow morning." So saying, the driver extracted a business card and gave it to Hal. "My name is Jonas. May I ask yours, sir?"

"Hal."

"Aha! Mr. Hal, you are my true friend now." And with that Jonas climbed into his taxi and drove away.

Hal remained in the desolate street, gazing at his surroundings. The darkness and the impassive accumulation of snow made everything look the same; nothing distinctive caught his eye. Still, Hal remained where he was, looking about blankly. Finally he hefted his suitcase and pushed open the door to the Hotel Užupis.

CHAPTER 2 The People of Hotel Užupis

Hotel Užupis was an ordinary European inn consisting of a lounge on the ground floor and guest rooms on the two stories above. The front door opened onto the dim lounge. Someone was singing, but Hal couldn't identify what kind of voice it was. A soprano? No, definitely not. Curious about the unusual timbre, Hal glanced about. A cloud of cigarette smoke hovered over a sea of heads—the lounge was full. Hal had encountered few people on his way here from the airport, and was taken aback by this sudden throng.

The voice was coming from a stage at the far end of the lounge, where a raw-boned man sang, accompanying himself on some sort of medieval instrument. In the middle of the lounge several couples danced slowly to the music.

The peculiar thing was, this place chock-full of people was muted except for the music. At first glance Hal thought it was a recital. But then he saw that most of the people looked gloomy, were preoccupied with the dancers, and silently sipped their drinks and smoked their cigarettes—not at all a recital audience. Finally Hal spotted a vacant table and settled himself there.

The next thing he knew, those nearby were gazing at him— at his large suitcase, his rare Asian features, and the snow coating his hair and shoulders. Especially curious were the five men and women drinking at the nearest table. One of them, a thirty-something woman, looked startled at the sight of him. She had a pale face, huge eyes, and hair so black it intensified the whiteness of her skin.

A boyish waiter appeared. Was a room available? Hal asked. Fortunately there was. Then, as Hal glanced nervously about the lounge, wondering what to drink, a massive man with a dark red beard showed him a glass containing a bright red liquid and gave a thumbs-up gesture. Taken with the man's playful expression, his beaming smile, his manner, Hal asked the waiter what the beverage was.

"*Pálinka.*"

"I'll have one."

No sooner had he said this than the men and women at the next table erupted with laughter, Redbeard signaling *okay!* with thumb and forefinger and nodding in satisfaction.

Aha, *pálinka* was their word for wine. Hal responded with a slight nod and a grin.

No one at the next table had yet spoken to Hal. Were they too shy to speak up to a foreigner who looked different? And yet the way they stole glances at him and whispered to one another told Hal they were very curious. The one who stood out the most was the startled woman with the huge eyes. She alone remained silent, smoking her cigarette in a deliberate manner. But her huge eyes kept returning to Hal, so he had no doubt she was aware of him.

The waiter returned with a room key and a glass of *pálinka*. Should he take Hal's suitcase upstairs? "No," said Hal, clutching the handle and drawing the suitcase close. "I can do it."

"As you wish," said the waiter. But as he was leaving, Hal detained him with a question.

"How did this hotel get its name?"

The waiter shrugged.

Hal tried again: "When was it built?"

The waiter shrugged again. "I really don't know anything about it. You'd have to ask the owner."

So saying, the waiter left for the bar, where he began speaking with a heavy-set, middle-aged man, gesturing a couple of times toward Hal. The man said something to the waiter, stealing glances at Hal. That must be the owner. The waiter returned.

"You ask why it's called Užupis? And how old it is? He doesn't know either. It's changed owners several times. But I do know it has been here at least two hundred years. Because Napoleon came through when he invaded Russia. And he lodged his cavalry officers here. You can look it up."

One of the women at the adjoining table tittered, another thirtyish woman, wearing glasses with angular black rims. The glasses made her look formidable and intelligent to Hal, who wondered if she was a high school mathematics teacher. Her tittering told him there was nothing credible in what the waiter had said. Hal thanked the young man anyway. "You're welcome," the waiter said with a sheepish grin before scurrying off. As soon as he was gone, the schoolmarm with the black-rim glasses leaned toward Hal.

"What he told you is a lie. This hotel was not built until after Lithuania became independent, with money from the Russian mafia, I'm sure. When he sees Japanese tourists like you, he likes to cook up extravagant stories."

Hal nodded—it made sense. "But I'm not Japanese and I'm not a tourist. I'm on my way to the Republic of Užupis and just laying over here."

The woman was dubious. "You're on your way *where?*"

"The Republic of Užupis."

At this she burst into a cackle. Noticing the others at the table staring at her uncomprehendingly, she offered an explanation in Lithuanian—after which they too erupted in laughter. The commotion attracted the attention of other parties. One person alone kept aloof—the woman with the pale face and huge eyes, smoking her cigarette.

Hal was bewildered—why was he a laughingstock all of a sudden?

The woman in the black-rimmed glasses explained: "This is Užupis; you are here, in the Republic of Užupis." She cackled again, while the rest of the group, all except the woman with the huge eyes, waited for Hal to react, managing with difficulty to contain their laughter.

Hal shrugged. Why weren't they taking him seriously?

A man with black hair and dark eyes—late twenties? early thirties?—joined the gathering. "I hope you will forgive us if we appear rude. But please do not misunderstand—there is a reason for our laughter."

Maybe it was the dark eyes, but Hal felt this man took him at face value, and he sounded like a sensible sort. Also, he had a better grasp of English than the others.

"The people of this city call this particular area Užupis—it means 'the other side of the river.' It is the most run-down area in

Vilnius. As a joke, the struggling artists who live here began calling it the Republic of Užupis. They even wrote a Declaration of Independence and established April Fool's Day as their Independence Day. Every year they celebrate it—the entire city knows about it—the Lithuanian president himself takes part in the festivities. So we could not help laughing when you said you were going to the 'republic.'"

Hal remained silent. Observing his sour face, Black Rims began cackling again. Hal waited for her to stop before speaking.

"That's interesting—a bogus Republic of Užupis. But where I'm going is not a joke, it's the actual Republic of Užupis." With that, Hal pulled the postcard from his pocket and displayed it. "This was mailed from the actual Republic of Užupis."

The black-and-white photograph on the postcard showed an elegant, venerable castle seemingly rising from a lake. It appeared to be made of marble slabs, and the architecture was exquisite. Flying from a tower was a flag, but of what domain it was impossible to tell. Sprawling in the distance were mountains clad with permanent snowfields, reminiscent of the Alps. The worn corners of the postcard attested to its age.

The man with the dark eyes examined the image and, unable to identify the castle, shrugged.

"That's the castle of the president of the Republic of Užupis," Hal pointed out. "It says so there." And indeed, printed in small letters at the corner of the card were the words "President's Castle, Republic of Užupis." Black Rims, inspecting the postcard with Dark Eyes, had stopped laughing.

Dark Eyes showed the postcard to his companions, explaining in Lithuanian, and Red Beard, together with the bony, blond-haired man next to him, leaned over to examine it. The woman with the huge eyes remained aloof, smoking her cigarette.

Finally Red Beard gave a big shrug. The bony, blond-haired man looked up and asked, "Trakai?" Red Beard shook his head vigorously.

"Where is Trakai?" Hal asked Dark Eyes, who was close beside him.

It was Red Beard who responded, slowly wagging his right index finger in Hal's face and saying with a heavy accent, "No, not Trakai."

Red Beard's attempt at English drew a hearty laugh from his companions.

"There is a medieval castle about thirty kilometers from here," Dark Eyes explained. "It's called Trakai. But it is not the castle in this photo. Trakai is made of red brick, but this one looks like marble, does it not? And Lithuania has no mountains. On top of everything else, the flag is different—it is not the Lithuanian flag."

Hal turned the postcard over. "You can see the flag better here," he said, indicating the stamp, which showed a bosomy woman from the waist up, against the background of the flag, which was still unidentifiable. The woman resembled Jurgita, from the airport.

Dark Eyes examined the stamp, then showed it to the others, who merely cocked their heads and shrugged—except for Red Beard, who exclaimed in wonder, apparently at the beautiful woman in the stamp. This drew a burst of laughter from his companions, followed by a round of chiding.

"Well, it seems that the Republic of Užupis where you are going is different from the Užupis we know," said Dark Eyes in a serious tone.

Hal felt like a traveler who has suddenly lost his way.

"Why did you come here anyway?" said Dark Eyes. "This is Lithuania, not the Republic of Užupis."

"Because I've heard that one gets to the Republic of Užupis through Vilnius. You take a taxi across the border. It's written here on the postcard." Hal indicated the text.

Dark Eyes peered at the words. Unable to read the unfamiliar writing, he sighed theatrically.

"If you want to take a taxi across the border, this is the place," said Black Rims. "So if it is the Republic of Užupis you seek, this is it." She had a mischievous smile, as if she might burst out cackling again at any moment. But when she saw Hal frown, she managed to stifle her laughter, and, for the time being, the five of them ceased talking about Hal.

Morose, Hal picked up his glass of *pálinka*. At the next table Red Beard responded by holding his glass high. Hal did likewise then downed his drink.

The *pálinka* was stronger than he had expected—powerful in fact. He made a face, drawing another burst of laughter from the group.

Red Beard extended a welcoming hand. "My name is Laurynas—what is yours?"

Hal told him, and they shook hands.

"Hal! Welcome to Lithuania!" said the man.

The next to greet Hal was Black Rims. "My name is Aistė." And then in English: "Welcome to the Republic of Užupis!" Her expression was as mischievous as ever.

Hal took her hand. Then Dark Eyes introduced himself as Alvydas, and the bony man with the blond hair, sitting next to red-bearded Laurynas, introduced himself as Marius. Finally, the woman with the huge eyes spoke one word—Vilma, her name.

As Hal shook hands with each in turn, Alvydas suggested he join them at their table. And soon he was settled among them, his suitcase and empty glass close at hand.

"Where are you from?" said Aistė, who was next to him.

"I'm from Han," said Hal. The response drew looks of surprise from everyone.

"Hun," murmured Marius. "Heavens—that is a long way from here."

"Hun," said Laurynas. "Great country!" Han, it seemed, was pronounced "Hun" in Lithuanian.

"Popa Tchiang," murmured Aistė. Was she referring to the world-famous Han actor Chang Popa?

They discussed this actor and then carried on about this and that, the conversation revolving around how large and amazing a country Han was.

"But I'm more fond of Užupis," Hal interjected.

"Why exactly are you going there?" Alvydas asked.

"I was born there. I'm a citizen of Užupis," said Hal, taking from his pocket an old black-and-white photograph. In it was a middle-aged man in full dress uniform, sitting stiff and stern, a medal pinned to his chest. Next to him sat a woman whose clothing bespoke refinement. Standing in front of the man and woman were a boy of six or seven and a girl who looked a couple of years younger. And behind the middle-aged man and the woman was a younger man, tall and with a stylish mustache, striking a pose for the camera. Judging from their attire and the elegant background, they were a dignitary and his family at the turn of the twentieth century.

"That gentleman is my father," said Hal. "He was the Republic of Užupis ambassador to Han. That was a long time ago, of course. And while he was posted in Han, Užupis, my fatherland, was forcibly occupied by the surrounding countries. My father was never able to go back there and had to live out his life in Han as an exile. But now that Užupis, my fatherland, is independent, I am going back there."

By now Aistė was no longer joking. "So there really is a Republic of Užupis and we know nothing about it?"

Laurynas picked up on her question: "It is true—many countries are free now. Our Lithuania too, you know. So maybe there is an Užupis, maybe it is free."

Hal identified the remaining individuals in the photo, pointing out each in turn: "This lady is my mother, this is my sister, and this is me."

"That cute young boy is you?" said Aistė in wonder, glancing back and forth between Hal and the boy in the photo.

"And this gentleman is my uncle," Hal continued. "He's a poet. He may still be alive, I'm not sure … The photo was taken in Užupis. And afterward, the four of us, everyone except my uncle, left for faraway Han."

Alvydas interpreted for Laurynas and for Marius, who, like his companion with the red beard, had limited English.

"This is something that Vladimir Shatunovsky could tell us about," muttered Laurynas.

Alvydas nodded. "You're right! For matters like this, Vladimir Shatunovsky is the one to ask."

"Ah yes," said Hal. "I seem to remember my father mentioning a man by that name. Was he the playwright?" But the next moment he cocked his head skeptically. "No, he wasn't a playwright. I think he was supposed to be the conductor of the Užupis Symphony Orchestra."

This time it was Alvydas who looked skeptical. No, he probably wasn't a conductor either.

"Well, if he's not a playwright or a conductor," said Hal, "then maybe he's a different person with the same name. If he's the Shatunovsky my father mentioned, then I think he had a limp. He had polio as a child."

"That's correct!" exclaimed Alvydas. "Vladimir has a limp. Whether from polio I do not know. So you know him too? He is a great scholar. There is no person in Lithuania who does not know who Vladimir is. He will know if there is in fact a Republic of Užupis, and if so, where it is."

"Yah," faltered Laurynas in his clumsy English, "only one thing Vladimir not know—women."

The others burst out laughing. Hal joined in, without knowing what was so funny. Vilma had still not uttered a single word, and now she looked worried.

"You should go see Vladimir," Aistė told Hal, now sounding sincere.

"But how? I'm a stranger."

Marius responded in Lithuanian. Aistė interpreted for Hal: "He says Vladimir is going to a party tonight at Eigis's. You can meet him there."

Alvydas joined in: "We are going too—that is why we have met here. You can join us if you wish. Then you can meet Vladimir Shatunovsky."

"But how far is it?" said Hal, worried.

"Close," broke in Laurynas. "Very close. We walk. Five minutes."

"But I wasn't invited," said Hal hesitantly.

"No problem," said Aistė and Laurynas simultaneously in English. "No problem."

All of a sudden the music became loud and cheerful—a lively dance tune had replaced the weepy solo on the medieval instrument. People flocked to the middle of the lounge to dance.

Just then the door to the lounge opened and half a dozen men and women entered, swaying to the music, their heads covered with snow.

The newcomers swarmed to where Alvydas and his party sat, and each made a show of shaking hands and saying hello. Everyone seemed to know everyone else.

Among the new arrivals the most outgoing was a hefty young man with glasses. Extending a paw-like hand to Hal, he introduced himself enthusiastically as Andrė.

Hal accepted the offered hand. "I am Hal."

Because of the music the other man seemed not to understand. Drawing close to Andrė, Alvydas practically shouted in his ear.

"Oh! Welcome to Lithuania, Hal!" shouted Andrė as he shook Hal's hand vigorously. Then, producing a flask, he filled Hal's empty glass, raised the flask high, and cried out, "*Kampai!*"

Surrounded by unfamiliar people and feeling overwhelmed, Hal responded with a "*Kampai!*" and drained his drink.

"Good!" shouted Andrė in English as he gave Hal a pat on the back. "Good!"

Alvydas again drew close to Andrė and spoke loudly into his ear. Andrė nodded repeatedly and, when Alvydas was done, shouted to Hal, "*Amigo!* Let us be off, my friend from Hun, we are off to Eigis's."

"Now?" asked Hal.

"Sure!" cried Andrė. "We will have a wild night." And then, addressing the others in English rather than Lithuanian, "Let us be off!"

Alvydas and his party jumped to their feet. Hal did likewise, gathered his suitcase, and followed the others outside.

CHAPTER 3 Chez Eigis

André and his group made their rambunctious way down the dark streets. The snow had given way to fog so thick they could scarcely see beyond their noses. To complicate matters, the streets in this venerable city were a labyrinth, with nary a street light to mitigate the blackness. Alone in these streets a first-time visitor would most certainly get lost. And so to make sure he could find his way back, at every corner Hal eyed the street sign and any distinctive buildings he could see.

André threw an arm around Hal's shoulder. "Beautiful, is it not?"

"Very beautiful," said Hal, not sure what André was referring to.

Satisfied with Hal's response, André launched into an animated spiel. His English was a challenge to understand, but Hal gathered from the repeated mention of Napoleon that the great man had once lived here, and had caught some kind of disease in the process. One particular Hal did understand was that Vilnius—the old town, that is—had been designated by UNESCO as a Cultural Heritage Site. "It makes sense," said Hal.

The group had just crossed a square and were passing a cathedral when an old woman squatting there sprang to her feet, scurried up to Hal, and began pleading with him. Hal could only gape at the woman, wondering why he was being targeted.

"Do not worry," said Aistė beside him. "She is a beggar, and you are a foreigner."

Hal made the connection, drew a banknote from his pocket, and gave it to the woman. He had heard, coming from the cathedral, the murmurs of a mass, and the beggar woman must have been waiting for the celebrants to emerge.

"*Ach'o! Ach'o!*" said the woman, overcome with gratitude. She rewarded Hal by making the sign of the cross and kissing his hand. The next thing Hal knew, two more beggars had run up to him. André barked at them, trying to shoo them away, but they clung desperately to Hal, pleading with him. Hal gave each of them a banknote.

"You're either a millionaire or you don't know any better, handing out a hundred *litas* each," scolded Aistė.

Hal felt compelled to explain: "That grandmother reminds me of my mother. She used to say that virtuous deeds earn countries for friends—it's an Užupis proverb."

"But if it becomes known that you are handing out a hundred *litas* each," Alvydas admonished him, "then every beggar in Vilnius will be after you."

Vilma alone remained silent, her huge eyes in their pale face observing Hal's every movement.

Suddenly a car parked on the street blared at the pedestrians passing innocently by. Someone in the group gave the bumper a swift kick, which only drew a louder clamor from the alarm. The others burst into laughter.

Eigis was a large, good-natured man in his mid-fifties. With an exuberant shout he welcomed André and his boisterous group of invaders. Hal didn't understand Eigis's greeting but imagined it to be something like "Where have you been, my cockeyed friends!" Their host greeted each of the group with a handshake and then, when Hal's turn arrived, he switched to English and said, "I do not believe we have met, my friend."

Hal broke into a grin. "This particular drunken friend flew into Vilnius only a few hours ago."

This response was evidently to Eigis's liking, and with an ebullient smile he gave Hal a pat on the back. Alvydas followed with a lengthy introduction, their host nodding repeatedly, and when he was done, Eigis said in English, "Welcome, Mister Hal, Welcome! Drink up while you can—Vladimir Shatunovsky will be here soon. Here in Lithuania we make enough vodka for our thirsty, far-flung guests."

So there Hal was, at a party he had never planned on attending.

He followed André and the others into a large foyer, where

he was confronted with a most peculiar sight. Some thirty men and women had gathered around something or other. There was none of the music and laughter you would expect to hear at a party. A stifling silence pervaded the room.

Hal's first thought was that the people were watching an arm-wrestling match, or perhaps a high-stakes card game. But if it were arm wrestling, where were the cheers from the spectators? And if gambling, where were the shouts of jubilation, the groans of lamentation? But there were no voices, only thick clouds of cigarette smoke.

"Good God," Alvydas muttered to himself. "This is pathetic."

Overcome by curiosity, Hal peered over the shoulders of the others. The next moment his jaw dropped, his face hardening in consternation.

Inside the circle was a small table and, resting on it, a revolver. Facing each other across the table were two glum young men. The onlookers waited with bated breath.

The man on the left picked up the revolver, gave the cylinder a sharp spin, and put the end of the barrel to his temple. Hal closed his eyes. He heard a distinct click—the gun had not fired. The observers broke out in a chorus of oohs and aahs, and with a sigh of relief the man with the revolver set it on the table. Then he quaffed the shot of vodka that sat before him. The man across from him closed his eyes in resignation. A third man, who appeared to be supervising the proceedings, filled the second man's shot glass. The second man's eyes opened and he took the vodka and considered it—his last shot of vodka ever? He brought it to his lips, threw back his head, and drank. Tension coursed through the crowd.

Finally the second man picked up the revolver. He spun the cylinder hard, like the first man, and, deadly solemn, put the muzzle to his temple. Just then a woman giggled. The man with the revolver likewise broke into laughter, then turned the gun on the woman and fired. This brought laughter from all, and the man then fired at random among them, each shot producing only the snap of the hammer against an empty chamber. When some of the "victims" sprawled out on the floor, Hal finally realized the gun wasn't loaded.

His tight lips relaxed into a smile.

The master of the house removed the revolver from his impetuous guests and went upstairs with it, and suddenly the house was booming with music. Strobe lights flashed and the guests danced, bodies swaying in abandon. Adding to this the clapping of hands and squeals of delight, and the mood of the party had changed utterly.

Hal was reluctant to join in the merrymaking. Standing off to the side, wine glass in hand, he watched the others dance. Several of the guests, curious about the Asian man, ventured near and tried to initiate a conversation, but their limited English proved an obstacle. A young man who said he had majored in computer science managed to start a dialogue of sorts, saying he had learned enough at the university to write a decent program, but because programmers in Lithuania didn't enjoy the same esteem as those in Hal's country of Hun, the people here were ignorant of his true value and he couldn't get a job. Hal soon lost interest in the dejected young man's tale of woe.

Also curious about him were three young women, barely out of their teens, planted in a row on a couch across the room. They seemed to find in the mysterious Asian man a source of wonder, and they kept up a constant chatter punctuated with giggles and glances in Hal's direction. All three were pretty and vivacious, but none ventured toward Hal to talk or dance. And Hal was not in the mood for flirting, preferring instead to keep an eye out for Vladimir Shatunovsky, who was expected at any moment.

Alvydas, Laurynas, Aistė, Marius, and Andrė of the oversize glasses had not forgotten Hal, and they tried to make sure he didn't feel left out. Whenever Andrė spotted him he would cry out, "Here you are, my friend Hal from Hun—it is a splendid night, yes?" But the way he bustled about, shaking everyone's hand and greeting them all in a similar tone, it was clear he was not going out of his way to look after Hal. Red-bearded Laurynas and desiccated, blond-haired Marius made a point of offering Hal food and drink, but their limited English kept their encounters short. Before long Marius discovered a doll-like Polish woman named Namunei. But while Marius was captivated with Namunei, she was more curious about Hal. Approaching, she peppered him with questions about Hun, asked what had brought him to Lithuania, wondered if he was married or single. But Hal didn't reciprocate, in spite of her comely looks and lovable demeanor, so she transferred her attention to a foreign correspondent from a German newspaper and clung to his side, while Marius, equally inept in German, could only hover nearby.

Sharp Aistė proved a big hit. Every once in a while she would greet Hal in French—"*Ça va?*" or "*Amusez-vous?*"—but soon she would be surrounded by admirers—Mark, a sturdy, handsome staffer at the American embassy; Jerome, a producer for a French television network; Simonas, a member of the Lithuanian National Assembly. Before long she too seemed to have forgotten that Hal even existed.

Black-eyed Alvydas was the only one to keep Hal company, and it was he who took Hal on a tour of the house. It was a splendid mansion, but it was showing signs of fatigue, and the elegant design was compromised by a complicated layout and an interior so dark that the detailed craftsmanship couldn't be appreciated. And because it was too commodious to heat, in winter everything above the second floor was closed off.

It must be a very old house, Hal said when he and Alvydas had finished. Yes, it dates from the seventeenth century, replied Alvydas. Then Eigis must be quite wealthy, said Hal. Alvydas shrugged as if to say, *Not really*. Then how could he own such a huge mansion? Hal asked. Alvydas lowered his voice to an undertone: "He is not a rich man—he is a dealer." Seeing Hal's uncomprehending expression, Alvydas explained. When Lithuania was occupied, the commanding officer of the occupying forces had lived here. After liberation, Eigis pulled some strings, snatched up the masterless estate, and made it his own. Hal nodded. After liberation, Alvydas continued, Eigis got in on the ground floor of the currency exchange business. He found he had a taste for it, and parlayed his profits into ownership of the Lithuania Free Newspaper Company, but lately he was being crowded out by competition funded by the Russian mafia, so his currency exchange business had declined and the newspaper was showing red ink every month, causing Eigis considerable hardship. If the home had been built in the seventeenth century, asked Hal, then who had lived here before Lithuania was occupied? Alvydas replied that he wasn't sure of the specifics, but had heard that a noble family had lived here before the occupation, and that when Lithuania was communized by the Soviets this storied family had exiled themselves to some far-flung land so their whereabouts were now unknown.

Just then, friendly Alvydas was whisked away by several guests who had just been introduced to Hal as members of the Lithuanian National Theater, and who now seemed anxious to speak with Alvydas. And that's when Hal learned that Alvydas was a playwright as well as a producer of plays. Before going off with the actors Alvydas urged Hal to enjoy the party—he would let him know when Shatunovsky had arrived.

Hal was not alone for long. A forlorn-looking man in his thirties came up and introduced himself as Rimas, a musician from Minsk, in Belarus. Although Lithuania and Belarus were neighboring countries, Rimas, like Hal, was a foreigner here, and perhaps he hadn't found anyone he felt comfortable with. Hal wondered if the man was partly Asian—he had bushy hair that was not quite black, dusky brown skin, and a pointed beard that reminded Hal of Genghis Khan. He was slow of speech but his English was intelligible, and something about his expression and tone of voice radiated sincerity.

Hal asked what kind of music the man played. Traditional Belarus music, answered Rimas, who then produced a postcard with a photo of several musicians playing instruments unfamiliar to Hal. Rimas pointed himself out in the photo, playing a harp-like instrument. But the Rimas in the photo was so much younger and more fashionably dressed than the Rimas before him that Hal was skeptical. And the instrument was definitely not a harp, though it might have resembled one.

Hal examined the photo before asking if the ensemble was now performing in Vilnius. No, Rimas replied, he was by himself—

he visited Vilnius around this time every winter. Then perhaps he had family, relatives, or friends here? asked Hal. Rimas paused before replying that he did have a friend in Vilnius, and that he always stayed with this friend, but he hadn't come to Vilnius to see this friend. He then asked what had brought Hal to Lithuania. Hal replied that he was passing through on his way to the Republic of Užupis. This brought a nod of comprehension from Rimas. Had he heard of the Republic of Užupis? asked Hal. Indeed he had, said Rimas; it was one of the countries, along with Belarus, Ukraine, Lithuania, Latvia, Estonia, and others, that had recently regained independence.

"Rimas!" said Hal. "So you've heard of it. Could you tell me what you know?"

Rimas raised an eyebrow in response to Hal's elation, but continued: "Well, the Republic of Užupis has a long history; just consider how far it spread southwest of here—Lithuania, Latvia, Estonia for starters; Poland, Romania, Belarus, even Ukraine—they were all part of Užupis. Of course by the time of independence it had shrunk to something as small as Lithuania."

"Rimas—where exactly is Užupis?" When Rimas responded with the same uncomprehending expression, Hal hastened to explain: "I know, it's difficult to understand, a man showing up in Lithuania saying he's going to Užupis and then asking where Užupis is; I must seem kind of pathetic and helpless. Still..."

Rimas nodded and then said, as if thinking out loud, that in Belarus he had heard people speak of the Republic of Užupis—and there were still people who spoke Užupis, it was an unusual language—and had heard it was located somewhere near the border of Lithuania and Belarus.

Before Hal knew it, Vilma, with her pale face and huge eyes, was standing beside him. He realized he hadn't seen her since their arrival. Rimas, startled, fell silent. Hal wanted to hear more from Rimas and gave Vilma scarcely a glance. But she was not to be deterred. She gazed at Hal as if he were a long-lost friend, and with all the affection she could muster she asked him to dance.

"Vilma, I'm talking with my friend Rimas from Belarus—it's very important."

But Vilma stood her ground. Draping her arms about Hal's neck, she led him to where the others were dancing. Hal glanced back; Rimas's face had hardened. *Wait*, he motioned to Rimas, as he and Vilma danced a tango. But when next he glanced back, Rimas was nowhere to be seen.

"Where did Rimas go?" Hal asked once the song was over.

"Do not worry about him—he is somewhere," Vilma said, taking Hal by the arm and leading him down a long, dark hallway, where she sat him on a bench. She returned shortly with two glasses of champagne.

"You are light on your feet," said Vilma, beaming with pleasure.

Hal shrugged.

Farther down the hall a couple were kissing. Was that Namunei the Polish doll, and the German correspondent?

"You should not trust Vladimir Shatunovsky," said Vilma.

Hal gave her an inquiring look.

"You should not meet him," she added.

"Why not?" Hal managed.

"Why not? Because he detests foreigners. He is a fascist."

"Is that the only reason?"

Vilma looked troubled—how to explain to the Asian gentleman? "If you are a foreigner, he is bound to hurt you in some way."

"But how?"

Vilma was silent for a time. "Not that I have any direct experience with him. But I heard that one foreigner he met ended up killing himself."

Hal shrugged, then waited in vain for Vilma to elaborate. "I don't understand. Am I not supposed to meet him on account of some vague rumor? It's not that I have important business with him—I just want to see what he knows about Užupis."

"Are you really thinking about going to Užupis?" She sounded nervous and looked overwrought.

"Of course—it's my fatherland."

Vilma heaved a disheartened sigh. "And of course I cannot blame you for going there—if it's your homeland. But you must not ask Shatunovsky about Užupis." Seeing that Hal didn't understand, she continued. "Naturally you will ask me why not. And I shall say to you again that he is a fascist and he detests foreigners. And you will ask me again if that is the only reason. And I shall tell you again that another foreigner asked him about Užupis and that foreigner killed himself. And the result of all this? You will not believe me." Vilma looked terribly sad.

Hal for his part was terribly dubious. Silently he regarded Vilma.

"Poor stranger," Vilma said, taking Hal's hand. "You know nothing about this country. There is no one here for you, no one to help you—truly no one. But worry not." After a pause she continued. "Tomorrow you will come for me. To ask my help. You can come for me anytime. I shall help you. I shall protect you. And if you wish, I shall be your friend. A friendly friend you can be absolutely open with, like a wife."

Patiently Hal asked, "Why do you want to help me?"

"Why?" Vilma considered this. "Because you are different from other people. You're honest, like all who wish to go to Užupis."

"You mean you've met others who wanted to go to Užupis?!"

Vilma took Hal's hands and placed them against her cheeks. Tears welled up in her huge eyes.

Just then they heard a piano. It was playing a dolorous, solemn sonata.

"Where's that music coming from?" Startled, Hal looked in both directions.

Vilma acted as if she hadn't heard it.

Hal rose, enchanted. Vilma's resentful eyes followed him until he had disappeared back up the hall.

Back at the party, Hal found small groups of guests chatting or dancing. But a quick look around revealed no piano. Hal returned to the hallway. Vilma was still there, enveloped in gloom, and farther down, Namunei and the German, leaning back against the wall, were locked in a passionate kiss. Still the piano played.

Hal threw open the first door he saw—a kitchen. A group of men and women sat around a table, giddy on marijuana. One of the men, more exhilarated than the rest, was rocking his head from side to side. In the corner sat a couple, eyes fixed affectionately on each other. The man stroked the inside of the woman's black stocking-clad thigh.

Hal crossed the kitchen and went out to a patio, where some of the others were having a smoke. Among them was Laurynas. Snow was still coming down. "Hey—my friend from Hun!" called the red-bearded man, beckoning Hal with an elaborate gesture. Outside, the sound of the piano was even more sonorous.

"Nice night, yes?" Hal recognized André by his large glasses.

But there was no time to linger. The music was growing more fervent and Hal had to find it.

"Where is it coming from?" Hal asked no one in particular. Laurynas seemed not to have caught the question. Hal stepped off the patio and craned his neck toward the second floor. There, right above the patio. Hal rushed back inside—through the kitchen, down the hall, and back to the foyer. The guests were still dancing, or else chattering away. He spotted a staircase and bounded up the steps, his sudden appearance drawing a round of titters from the perky triplets perched on them.

The second floor was also divided by a long hallway. Hal followed it, the music growing ever more impassioned, swelling into a crescendo. He quickened his pace and finally he arrived at a spacious parlor, apparently a counterpart to the foyer downstairs. Across the parlor was a large picture window affording an excellent view of the falling snow. To one side was a grand piano, and playing it a woman of surpassing beauty and grace. Hal flinched—the performer was none other than Jurgita, from the airport. Standing behind her, wine glass in hand, was a hefty middle-aged man.

The performance came to an end. Jurgita grew still, staring straight ahead, her face shrouded in sorrow.

"Bravo!" The man placed his wine glass on the piano and applauded.

Jurgita remained motionless, her doleful countenance reminding Hal of someone pining for a past that has forever been lost. The man kissed her cheek and the nape of her neck. Jurgita didn't move. The two of them seemed unaware of Hal, standing in the corner.

"Hal—Vladimir is here!" The shout came from Alvydas.

Now it was Hal who was still, observing Jurgita like a man in a trance.

Alvydas tapped Hal on the shoulder. "Now you can find out where Užupis is."

Startled, Jurgita looked their way. Her eyes made contact with Hal's, which were still fixed on her. The hefty man, still oblivious to Hal and Alvydas, kissed Jurgita's earlobe. Jurgita no longer seemed aware of him as she stared at Hal with rueful eyes.

"Let us go—Vladimir is waiting for you," said Alvydas, leading Hal off by the arm.

"Do you know what that was?" said Hal, referring to the music, his gaze still stuck on Jurgita.

Do you know who *that was?* was what Alvydas seemed to have heard. "Oh, that is the man who runs Danish Air—he is a friend of Eigis."

"Not the man," said Hal with a note of annoyance. "The music—did you recognize it? It's the Užupis national anthem."

CHAPTER 4 **Vladimir of the Silver Hair**

Hal followed Alvydas into a large study. The walls were lined with bookshelves packed with ancient tomes in ornate bindings. The shelves on the wall to the right flanked a pair of windows some three feet apart, the gap filled by a bust carved from white marble. The bust was of a man, his agonized face cupped in his hands.

Sitting at a large, rectangular table in the middle of the room was a silver-haired man in his sixties who looked very much out of sorts. This must be Vladimir Shatunovsky. Beside him, head drooping, was a younger woman. Hal wondered if she was intoxicated—perhaps that explained Vladimir's ill humor.

"Hi," said the silver-haired man in a staccato voice as he shook hands with Hal. For a man of his age he radiated vitality. His face had a ruddy glow and his eyes gave off a brilliant luster. His smile revealed ivory-white teeth and gums the crimson of coral.

After Hal and Vladimir had introduced themselves, the woman managed to lift her head and extend a hand.

"Hi there—I'm Sophie."

Hal took her hand, noticing that for a woman who was half Vladimir's age she was physically wasted. Once she must have been beautiful, but now her eyes were dark pits and her teeth were stained black. Was this the result of alcohol and tobacco?

"Sophie used to be a famous ballerina in France," said Alvydas as Hal shook hands with the woman.

Vladimir gazed in disgust at Sophie until Hal had seated himself.

"Alvydas has told me plenty about you—the man from Hun, looking for the Republic of Užupis, who heard from his father about gimpy old Shatunovsky. But who exactly is your father?"

Vladimir's English was clear and to the point. Hal felt he was sensing the man's words rather than hearing them. He told Vladimir his father's name.

Vladimir shrugged. "Can't say I've ever heard it. Probably some other Shatunovsky your father knew. There could be other

Shatunovskies besides me who walk with a limp."

"I guess so," said Hal. "Or maybe I misunderstood my father."

"Can you show Vladimir that photograph?" said Alvydas.

Hal pulled out the photo and Alvydas passed it to Vladimir.

"That's my father in the middle," said Hal as Vladimir studied the picture.

Vladimir gave the same shrug—the face was unfamiliar. "Is he still alive?"

"No, he passed away twenty years ago."

"How old would he be if he were still alive?"

Hal calculated briefly. "Seventy-seven, this year."

Vladimir spread his palms wide, as if everything had suddenly become clear. "That would make him twelve years older than me. So he couldn't have been a close friend of mine. For sure it's another Shatunovsky your father knew—some other Shatunovsky with a limp." He smiled, displaying his dazzling teeth and crimson gums.

In despair Hal produced several other photographs. They too were family shots, and one of them included a blond-haired girl who was playing a grand piano. The setting of this photo was like the room where Hal had just seen Jurgita—a parlor with a large picture window affording an excellent view of the falling snow. But Hal failed to notice this similarity. Or that the girl in the photo bore a startling resemblance to Jurgita. Nor did Vladimir or Alvydas comment on the photo.

In another photograph, taken in a study, people sat around a huge table engaged in conversation. The walls were lined with bookshelves packed with ancient tomes in ornate bindings. The wall to the right, as you looked at the photo, bore windows, the source of light for the scene. Prominent in the photo was the marble sculpture set between the windows, a bust of a man whose agonized face was cupped in his hands. The study was virtually identical with the room in which Hal now sat with Vladimir. But the three men failed to notice this.

Vladimir inspected another of the photographs.

"That man there is my father," Hal explained. "He was the

Užupis ambassador to Han at the time. The man beside him is my uncle—he was a poet. The tall boy standing in front of them is me, and the little girl with the blond hair is my cousin—the poet is her father."

The photo had been taken outdoors, at a summer resort. The two men wore white slacks and short-sleeve shirts; the boy wore shorts and a straw hat; and the girl was clad in a dress.

"It was taken when my family and I were at our summer villa in Gruzia. Back then the people of Užupis, most of them, liked to venture far afield for their summer vacation."

By now Vladimir was plainly bored.

"One thing I don't understand," broke in Alvydas, who was next to Vladimir, as he considered the photos. "Your cousin is a blond-haired Westerner, but you, your father, and your uncle are black-haired Asians—why is that?"

Hal nodded. "It's a long story."

But before he could explain, Vladimir cut him off. "So what's the point? Is there supposed to be proof in these photos of the existence of the Republic of Užupis?"

The questions intimidated Hal into a momentary silence. He considered. Then, removing a small box from his suitcase, he said, "If it's proof you're looking for, this should suffice." He opened the box to reveal a medal. "My father was awarded this medal by the president. You can see the lettering: 'President of the Republic of Užupis.'"

Alvydas took the box from Hal and showed Vladimir the medal. While Vladimir studied it with disdain, Hal hastened to add, "And—you can see the medal in the photographs, on my father's chest."

Vladimir didn't bother to look. "A medal in a photograph—now *that's* convincing." And then he shot to his feet, limped to one of the bookcases, and returned with a volume of an encyclopedia. "Take a look—see if you can find the Republic of Užupis. I'll bet you won't find a country by that name."

When Hal, bewildered, showed no interest, Alvydas began to leaf through the book.

"Of course," crowed Vladimir, "you might find it in the next edition, ten years from now—that is, if you finally manage to conjure up your Republic of Užupis."

Hal was at a loss.

Alvydas industriously perused the volume. "Did it ever occur to you what the word *užupis* means?" challenged Vladmir. "It's really quite simple—it means 'across the river.' It's not the name of a country."

Hal heaved a despondent sigh.

Next to Vladimir Sophie lifted her head from the table. "In France if you say 'užupis,'" she slurred, "it sounds like *où-je-pisse*, 'where I piss'—in other words, a potty."

Vladimir slapped her hard across the face. "Don't you ever shut up?" he shouted.

The force of the blow sent the woman tumbling to the floor. There she lay squirming, trying to get up.

Vladimir looked down at her. "Wretched French whore!"

Finally, the woman managed to grab hold of the table, pull herself up, and reclaim her seat, and there she sat meekly, eyes downcast.

There followed a brief, awkward silence, and then Vladimir carried on in a spirited voice as if nothing had happened: "I can't for the life of me understand it—why does a man like you come all the way here believing there's a country called Užupis? Whatever gave you that idea?"

Hal maintained a sullen silence.

"Or maybe it's the Užupis across the Vilnia River you're looking for," mocked Vladimir, "where the drunks live. On April Fool's Day they play their little game of proclaiming the independence of Užupis. Maybe that's what puts such wild notions into the heads of you naïve foreigners. If you need to, we can go over and say hello to them tomorrow."

"But there are many autonomous regions in Russia—couldn't Užupis be one of them?" asked Alvydas nervously. He sympathized with Hal.

"Sure," chided Vladimir. "And while we're at it we could have ourselves a tour of Siberia."

Alvydas tried again. "Perhaps there are records of a nation in history named Užupis?"

"Why not?" Vladimir shot back. "All we need is some brilliant anthropologist to find them—a set of Dead Sea Scrolls for the Republic of Užupis!" He guffawed, having made his point, his boisterous laughter both cheerful and narcissistic.

Hal began deliberately to put away the medal and the photos.

"Why do you foreigners come here saying you're looking for the Republic of Užupis?" Vladimir muttered to himself. "I just don't get it."

"You mean others have come looking for the Republic of Užupis?" Hal asked, looking Vladimir directly in the eye.

"Oh yes. Several years back. With Asian features, like you. From Kazakhstan or Uzbekistan, maybe. Or were they from Hun?"

"And what happened?" said Alvydas.

"They ended up dead. Wandered around Vilnius for a few days, saying they were going to the Republic of Užupis, and then they shot themselves."

"Why did they do *that*?" asked Alvydas, burning with curiosity.

"I don't know."

A leaden silence fell over them. And then a gunshot pierced the air.

"Who is it now!" Vladimir thundered, jumping to his feet. "Every time these idiots get together."

And then he was gone. Hal noticed his limp was more pronounced. Alvydas followed, and Hal was left at the table. He quickly finished re-stowing his belongings. Drunken Sophie, head still drooping, hadn't moved.

Hal returned to the main floor and found the guests in a state of agitation. Vladimir was looking about and loudly berating everybody. And then Eigis appeared at the top of the stairs. Down he came, a revolver held high for all to see, finger on the trigger, a broad smile on his face—his exaggerated movements apparently designed to ease the concerns of the startled guests and to calm the gathering. He barked out something. Vladimir shouted back at him. *What happened?* Hal imagined him saying. Or *Who shot whom?* Eigis responded with a grand gesture indicating the weapon had fired by mistake. Vladimir looked dubious and bawled out something else. Chagrined, Eigis tried again to explain, this time more urgently.

"What is he saying?" Hal asked Alvydas.

"He didn't know it was loaded."

Just then Jurgita, wearing a black overcoat, appeared at the top of the stairs. She began to descend, assisted by another woman. The party fell silent, including Eigis the host, who seemed resigned to the fact that no further explanation was necessary.

The guests parted for Jurgita. Absorbing their gazes, she made her way between them. Hal was observing her with the others, when she abruptly swung her pale face up; their eyes made contact. And then she had passed him and disappeared outside.

As soon as Jurgita was gone, Eigis shouted something to the effect that the commotion was over and all the guests should have a rollicking good time—or so Hal interpreted it. Cheerful music broke out and Eigis hastened upstairs, gun in hand. But the mood had turned oppressive, and in spite of the music no one was dancing. Instead the guests stood around in small groups speaking in hushed tones.

André found Hal again. "Beautiful night, yes?"

Hal shrugged.

"Do not be concerned. Something like this happens every year—it livens up Eigis's parties."

Hal grinned, and before long André had disappeared back into the crowd.

And sure enough, the guests soon resumed dancing and chattering away—they seemed to have forgotten the fuss. A short time later an old man with a medical bag appeared and proceeded upstairs, but no one seemed to pay him any attention.

On a whim Hal went upstairs to the parlor, where Jurgita had been playing the piano. The lights were still on but no one was there. Hal noticed bloodstains on the keyboard and carpeted floor.

He heard voices from the next room, which was accessed by

a door that was half-open. Concealing himself behind the door, Hal peeked into a bedroom. His eyes were drawn first to the hefty president of Danish Air, who sat on a couch, naked from the waist up. He had been shot in the shoulder and was being treated by the elderly doctor. Tossed over the armrest of the couch was a white dress shirt mottled with blood. Eigis's wife was assisting the doctor while Eigis himself fussed about, pacing the room. In his hand was an object wrapped in a white towel—the revolver, Hal guessed.

"Yow!" said the large man, making a face, to which the doctor said something Hal couldn't make out. But it seemed the wound was not so deep.

A short time later the patient said something to Eigis, who quickly responded by fishing out a pack of cigarettes, one of which he placed in the other man's mouth. He hastened to produce a lighter, but this required him first to set the towel-wrapped revolver on a table. The sight of the weapon disturbed his wife, who began to nag him. Eigis bobbed his head as if to say, *Yes, I know*, and once he had lit the wounded man's cigarette he took the revolver and came out from the bedroom into the parlor. Hal made sure he was safely hidden behind the door.

From his vantage point Hal saw Eigis scurry up a spiral staircase in the corner of the parlor and disappear into what Hal guessed was some sort of secret loft. Hal hesitated a moment, came to a decision, and followed Eigis up the staircase. There he saw a storage room for old knickknacks that must once have been a room where children studied their lessons. Eigis had rolled back the carpet and was lifting up one of the floorboards, evidently to hide the gun.

Hearing Hal enter, Eigis jerked his head up in alarm. "You can't come in here!" he huffed.

But Hal was unruffled. "Please—could you sell it to me?"

At first Eigis didn't understand. "Go—you shouldn't be here."

Hal sat down at a child's desk, produced a check, and filled it out. "Here—please give me the gun."

"What do you want with it?" asked Eigis with a look of suspicion.

"I want it for a souvenir—something to remember your party by."

Eigis gave Hal a dubious look, then found his reading glasses and examined the check. After he had looked back and forth several times between Hal and the amount written on the check, he finally spoke. "Well, I don't see why not, if that's what you really want. I guess it's all right if it's just a souvenir."

So saying, Eigis proffered the gun in its towel wrapper. Hal snatched the weapon and stuffed it in his coat pocket.

"But you mustn't tell anyone you bought it from me. You promise?" Eigis didn't sound at all comfortable with the arrangement.

"I promise," said Hal.

Only then did Eigis seem to relax. And as an afterthought, from a cabinet he produced a small box of ammunition and proclaimed in an expansive tone, "I'll throw this in as well—I won't be needing it anymore."

"Thank you," said Hal as he pocketed the box. "And by the way, this is a fine home you have. How long have you lived here, if I may ask?"

Eigis was puzzled.

"Well, if *I* may ask, why do *you* ask?"

Hal lapsed into thought before mumbling, as if to himself, "Oh, I don't know—it just feels like I've been here before."

Eigis shrugged. "Maybe you have."

Hal shrugged in his turn. "It's been a lovely night," he said, extending a hand.

"The pleasure is mine," said Eigis, shaking Hal's hand, "hosting a distinguished gentleman such as yourself."

These pleasantries concluded, Hal exited the room.

As he was making his way down the spiral staircase, Eigis called after him, "Do you really think this is a fine home?"

Hal looked back at Eigis, who was following him down the steps. "Why wouldn't it be?"

Eigis had to think about this. "Sure. Why wouldn't it? The thing is, at this time of year I have a hell of a time keeping it warm.

The price of oil in our country has skyrocketed."

"But," Hal blurted out, "originally this house wasn't heated by oil." The next moment he realized his mistake. But large Eigis seemed not to have understood, and Hal corrected himself: "Well, maybe it used to be heated by something else."

This time Eigis caught the drift. "That's my guess," he agreed, "oil heating probably didn't exist back then."

At the bottom of the spiral staircase, back in the parlor, Eigis extended his hand once again. "It's been a pleasure hosting such a distinguished gentleman."

"And I've had a lovely evening," said Hal as he shook hands one more time.

Downstairs the guests were dancing in abandon to a spirited tune. Who would have thought a gunshot had rung out earlier?

Hal scanned the room for Rimas but didn't see him. He made a circuit of the hallway, the kitchen, and the patio, but Rimas was nowhere to be seen. Perhaps he had gone home. Hal located his suitcase and left.

CHAPTER 5 **Nocturnal Encounters**

Outside it was still snowing. The dank, chilly air soon had Hal hacking. He went down a dark lane, and in no time he was lost. The alleys were a confused tangle, and in the darkness a stranger could hardly be expected to retrace a path he had traveled but once. Worse, at this late hour, with the snow falling, Hal saw no one to ask directions of.

Several times he turned back toward Eigis's, and each time he was foiled by a junction with another alley. And then he turned a corner and almost bumped into a figure looming in the dark, a middle-aged man who must have been six and a half feet tall. Hal flinched and began to step back. The man stood like a statue, motionless, gazing down upon him.

Hal's finger closed around the trigger of the revolver in his pocket as he looked up at the man. Thankfully the man didn't look to be a violent sort, didn't seem predatory or aggressive. Maybe when younger the man was different, but now he simply seemed worn out. His cheeks were cavernous and his shoulders slumped lifelessly. Hal wondered if the man was unemployed. Or perhaps he had been banished to Siberia back when Lithuania was part of the USSR. The rigid, solemn-faced man continued to gaze at Hal.

Convinced he was no threat, Hal relaxed his trigger finger and called out a hearty hello.

The man made no response, merely gazed down at Hal with vacant eyes, ghostlike. How long had the man been standing there? Hal wondered as he noticed the thick coating of snow on the man's head and shoulders.

"I'm lost," Hal shouted, and he forced a smile in an attempt to suppress the fear building inside him. "Could you show me the way to the Hotel Užupis?" When this brought no response, Hal decided to beat a hasty retreat from this strange man. "Well, no matter. It seems you don't speak English. And that's no crime. Not everybody gets to be born in England or the U.S."

So saying, he scurried toward the first alley he saw. Hurrying blindly along, he grumbled to himself, "Damn, so much snow."

"Hal? Is that you, Hal?"

Hal felt a shiver go up his spine as the words registered. They weren't English and they didn't sound like Lithuanian—they were Užupis!

Hal turned back but there was only the man at the corner. He couldn't believe that the words he had just heard had come from that stock-still figure. "Did you say something?" he shouted. Then he attempted to repeat the question in Užupis, but the words wouldn't come out.

"Hal—it's you, isn't it? You've come back, haven't you?" The same voice came from out of the darkness.

Hal could see that the man was looking his way, but was rooted in the same place as before. No, it couldn't have been him.

Still, Hal shouted back, "How do you know my name?" And again it was English that came out of his mouth. Although Hal recognized Užupis when he heard it, he had long forgotten how to speak it.

Again came the voice from out of the gloom: "My name is Urbonas. I knew you would come back." But the man still hadn't budged. Hal felt like he was speaking with a ventriloquist.

"Urbonas!" Hal called out, trembling half in delight and half in fear.

And then from the far end of the alley there appeared a patrol car, warning lights flashing. The man ducked out of sight.

"Just a minute!" Hal shouted. "Wait." But the man had vanished.

"Urbonas—Urbonas," Hal mumbled. As he peered with anxious eyes toward the gloom into which the man had disappeared, the patrol car crept toward him. It hovered close by, and Hal expected the patrolmen to stop to question the weird-looking foreigner with the huge suitcase in the snow-choked alley. But instead the car inched away, the police presumably lacking sufficient grounds to detain him. Nonetheless, Hal felt the full weight of their suspicion. He had no way of knowing that the presidential palace was not far off, and that the police frequently patrolled this area.

Hal remained where he was after the cruiser had passed. Perhaps Urbonas would return. Then again, what reason would he have to reappear? Standing mutely at the corner with the snow falling about him, Hal didn't look so different from Urbonas a short time before.

How long had he been waiting in the numbing cold? From the far end of the alley there appeared a shadow. "Urbonas!" Hal cried in delight. The shadow took the form of a man trudging toward him. The man didn't answer, but his plodding bespoke a most laborious task. Hal rushed toward him. But instead of Urbonas it was the man toting the huge grandfather clock—no wonder he looked so burdened.

Deflated, Hal came to a stop. The man proceeded in silence, taking no notice of him. Hal imagined a man compelled to carry his own casket to the grave.

When the man was no longer in sight, Hal resumed his own leaden pace. Had he come across a familiar street leading back to the hotel? No, the maze of alleys was taking him farther away. Worse, he was growing hypothermic, his exposure to the cold, damp air clouding his mental acuity.

And then he saw a familiar face.

"Rimas!" Hal screamed in elation. His friend must have been on his way home from Eigis's.

But there was no joy in Rimas's face. Instead he looked angry.

"Rimas! Help me, I'm lost! I have to get back to the Hotel Užupis, but I can't find my way."

Grudgingly Rimas replied, "You're going the wrong way—you need to go in the opposite direction."

"Rimas!" Hal pleaded, gripping Rimas's arm. "Don't leave me. I've been wandering for an hour and I'm freezing. Help me, please!"

Rimas merely regarded Hal with contempt.

"Rimas, did I do something wrong? Why are you looking at me like that? Is it because I left the party without saying goodbye? I tried to find you before I left, but I couldn't see you. So I left by myself. Don't be upset with me."

Hal's words had no effect on Rimas's anger. "I want an honest answer," he snapped. "What's your relationship with her? Are you sleeping with her or not?"

Hal was incredulous. "With who?"

"The girl you were dancing with—Vilma."

"Vilma? Am I sleeping with Vilma? Absolutely not." Rimas looked ambivalent.

"Whatever gave you that idea? I only arrived here seven hours ago, you know. I'm going to the Republic of Užupis. And lucky me, I get a low-down, cheating taxi driver. He takes me for an hour-long joy ride and guess where he dumps me—not the Republic of Užupis but the Hotel Užupis. I met Vilma in the lounge there—for the first time. And her friends—Alvydas, Laurynas, Marius, and Aistė. They took me to that party. And that's my relationship with Vilma."

Rimas finally began to soften. "The cab drivers in Minsk rip off foreigners too."

"Can we go somewhere warm?" Hal pleaded. "I'm freezing."

"I suppose," said Rimas, nodding. "Why not. But on one condition."

Hal rested his head against his savior's shoulder. "Anything you say—just as long as I can get out of this damn cold."

"Promise me," Rimas said resolutely. "Promise me you'll never lay a hand on Vilma."

"Of course. Not even a finger—I swear."

Finally Rimas relaxed. "All right, then, let's get you warmed up. Hold on to me," he said, securing Hal against him. They set off down the snowy alley, Hal's head glued to Rimas's shoulder. "Here, give me your suitcase."

Hal looked up anxiously. "It's all right, it's not that heavy." After a pause he explained: "Not that it contains anything of value. It's just that I feel leery of others handling it—some of my father's belongings are in there."

Rimas listened silently.

"For example—his tuxedo, his hat, his shoes, the things he wore when he was a diplomat. Not so special, I guess, but to me they're dear. All the memories of my family when they lived in Užupis are in that suitcase. I think you can understand."

Rimas remained silent.

"One more thing," Hal added. "His ashes are in there too. Before he passed on he asked me to bury his ashes in his homeland. That's why I need to carry it myself. Now does it make sense?"

Instead of replying, Rimas led Hal toward a small café at the next corner. As they went in, Rimas supporting him, Hal noticed a small sign—Café Mano.

Rimas found a table, then ordered soup for Hal and a vodka for himself.

Hal attacked the soup as soon as it arrived. Rimas, though, allowed his vodka to sit while he studied Hal. Hal slurped the hot soup, and eventually he perked up.

"Rimas," he said. "You saved me. I really appreciate it." A steady drip came from his nose.

Rimas produced a tissue and gave it to Hal. "Well, you're my friend—as long as you steer clear of Vilma."

"There must be a misunderstanding—I don't have any feelings for her," Hal hastened to explain. After seeing how Rimas took this, Hal continued: "Anyone can see she's attractive: her skin and those big eyes give her a mysterious beauty."

Rimas smiled, but the smile was fleeting and Hal noticed a lingering suspicion.

"She's pretty all right, but to me she feels like a cousin, nothing romantic. Besides, I came here to find Užupis, not to pick up women."

Finally Rimas grinned. "All right, you have convinced me. She does have a mysterious beauty. I have been in love with her the past ten years. But she does not know it." So saying, he downed his vodka. "Ten years ago Belarus and Lithuania were both part of the USSR. And during that time, the folk music group I belong to came to Vilnius frequently. I was thirty then and she was only seventeen. She looked like an angel, with her fair complexion and large eyes. From then on, I came here every winter. The first time I met her was during a winter just like this. But up to now I have never spoken a word to her, just watched her from a distance."

"So, a modern-day Dante." But Hal's drowsy eyes betrayed his lack of interest in Rimas's love story. His nocturnal wanderings and jet lag were starting to make him feel like a rag doll, and it was all he could do to keep his eyes open. Still, he managed to look up once or twice and keep the conversation going.

"If you love her so much, why not ask her to marry you? Maybe she needs you too."

Rimas said something, but it didn't register with Hal. As Rimas was taking pains to explain, Hal's head dropped to the table and he was fast asleep.

Rimas continued his story nonetheless, drinking a couple more vodkas. The next thing Hal knew, Rimas was shaking him by the shoulder. He was startled awake.

"You need to go to bed," said Rimas. "Now that you are warmed up, I will take you to your hotel."

Hal picked up his suitcase and lurched to his feet. He had intended to pay, but saw that Rimas had taken care of the bill. He thanked Rimas, saying he would treat him next time.

The two men set out once more through the snow-laden alleys. Warmed up sufficiently and refreshed by his brief nap, Hal felt lighter on his feet, while Rimas, a bit tipsy, was more unsteady.

At the hotel door, thinking Rimas might have crucial information about the Republic of Užupis, Hal, asked, "Why don't we meet tomorrow?" Rimas responded with a noncommittal nod. Hal tried again, more importunate this time: "Rimas, I don't feel right saying goodbye forever. How about this—tomorrow morning come by around eight and we'll have breakfast."

Rimas wore the same indecisive look.

"If eight is too early we can make it nine—or ten, even—it's all the same to me. What do you say?"

Seeing no change in Rimas's expression, Hal continued: "Or if it's too much of a bother, I can meet you where you're staying—can you give me the address of your friend from Belarus? We can do it that way, yes?"

Finally Rimas replied. "That would be a bit of a problem. My friend would not like that. I will see if I can come back here. But I am not promising anything."

"Why not?"

"I might have to take a bus to Kishinev—that is, unless there is too much snow."

"Kishinev?"

"Yes—it is the capital of Moldova. You get there by way of Warsaw, and in weather like this it takes three days."

Hal began to feel desperate.

"I have a younger brother," Rimas explained. "He's married to a Moldovan, and they live in Kishinev. I just heard that my brother is in the hospital—he has cancer. I need to see him one last time, and I have to talk with his wife, Donata, about what to do with their three children."

"I'm so sorry to hear that," said Hal. "But isn't there any hope? They say that if you treat it early enough, a complete cure is possible, even for cancer."

Rimas answered in a monotone: "I think it is too late. Then again, he probably will not die right away..."

Hal heaved a sigh. "All right, but if the snow keeps you here in Vilnius for the next few days, would you let me know? And if I've checked out, you could leave a message at the front desk—I'll come by now and then and check, and I'll leave you a message too."

Rimas nodded, then went off in the direction from which they had come. Hal followed his retreating form into the snowy distance.

A blond-haired girl in her early teens selling flowers tiptoed up to Hal and silently offered him a red rose. Her eyes sparkled with intelligence. Her customers must have been the tipplers emerging from the hotel bar.

"Aren't you freezing?" said Hal.

The girl seemed not to understand English, and once again held out the rose.

"It really is cold here," said Hal as he reached into his pocket. "But not in Užupis—it's nice and cozy there, even in winter."

"Tuh-ree *litas*," said the girl.

Hal interpreted this as three *litas*, took a 200-*litas* bill from his wallet, and offered it to the girl. "I don't suppose you've ever heard anyone speak of the Republic of Užupis?"

The girl looked dismayed, and Hal guessed she didn't have change. "But how could a girl like you know something not even the adults know? I don't need the change—why don't you run along now."

The girl said something in Lithuanian.

"I said, you keep it," said Hal.

The girl took the bill but didn't seem to know what to do with it. Hal made a reassuring gesture, but the girl was disbelieving.

"It's all right," said Hal, repeating the gesture. "Run along, now."

The girl finally seemed to understand. But she didn't seem pleased with her windfall and said something else in Lithuanian, a helpless look on her face.

"Don't mention it," said Hal, who assumed the girl was thanking him. "I won't need this money in the Republic of Užupis. And it's too cold here—I really don't like this country."

The girl didn't understand this and spoke once again in Lithuanian.

Hal entered the hotel and went straight up to his room. He sank down onto his bed and sat there motionless, waiting for his body to thaw all over again. Quite some time passed before he opened his suitcase, removed several of the articles, and arrayed them on the nightstand—the funerary photograph of his father, his father's medals, and the black wrapping cloth containing the urn with his ashes.

When he had arranged these items to his satisfaction he placed the rose from the girl atop the urn. Then he took out the revolver and placed it before the framed photograph.

Hal viewed the items he had displayed with such care. Then he undressed, got into bed, and closed his eyes. Only a short time had passed when he bolted upright. Taking the revolver from the nightstand, he fondled it, then touched the grip to his lips. He had rediscovered something valuable but long forgotten.

CHAPTER 6 Tomas, Prime Minister of Užupis

It was four in the morning when Hal awoke. He had slept scarcely three jet-lagged hours. He ought to catch a few more hours of rest, he told himself, but sleep proved elusive.

He flung the curtain aside and looked out the window. It was still snowing, but feebly—not enough to prevent Rimas from traveling by bus to Kishinev. There passed several hours of drudgery, Hal going back to bed to toss and turn, then rising again to gape out the window, repeating this process as he awaited dawn.

At eight o'clock it was still pitch dark. Hal went down to the front desk and asked if anyone had tried to contact him. No, no one, said the sleepy-eyed young man on duty. If someone came for him, said Hal, could he please be notified? Of course, said the young man. Back upstairs Hal went.

Nine o'clock arrived and still it was black outside. Hal went back down to the front desk to ask if he had had any callers. Once again the sleepy-eyed young man said no, and once again Hal returned to his room.

Not until almost ten did the dark begin to yield. Hal packed his suitcase and went downstairs. Hearing yet again that he had had no visitors, he requested a sheet of paper and wrote the following:

> *My good friend Rimas,*
> *If by chance you stay in Vilnius another day, I would be grateful if you could leave me your local address. I will check back here from time to time to see if you have left me a message.*
>
> *10:02 a.m.*
> *Your friend, Hal*
>
> *P.S. Vilma is indeed a woman of heavenly beauty.*

Leaving this message with the young man, Hal exited the hotel.

Morning left the city looking more desolate to Hal than it had the previous evening. Most of the buildings looked glum and distinctly the worse for wear, and quite a few looked abandoned. Walkways and motorways alike were sheets of ice, but snow removal was under way, judging from the occasional mound of dirty snow heaped on the side of the street.

The city was still overcast, and today it was shrouded as well, with barely thirty feet of visibility in any direction. Pedestrians emerged coughing from the fog to Hal's left and coughed their way back into the fog to his right. The sodden chill that characterized the weather here must have made the local people susceptible to pneumonia. Before he realized it, Hal was coughing along with them.

As Hal coughed his way through the murky streets, headed he knew not where, he came out onto a broad thoroughfare near the white building identified to him by the taxi driver the night before as City Hall. There he discovered a small restaurant, and in he went, deciding he had had enough of the bone-numbing chill and dampness. A boy with a shaved head and earrings was busy drying glasses.

"Hi!" said Hal. The boy made no reply. Was he a xenophobe? "Winter here is really something," Hal ventured in an attempt to dispel his awkwardness. But then he erupted in a spasm of coughing, drawing a smirk from the boy. Finding a seat near a window looking out onto the street, Hal ordered soup. At this early hour he had the restaurant to himself.

Through the window Hal saw that the feeble snowfall had resumed. People scurried along, hunched up against the frigid temperature, while vehicles with chains on their wheels rattled down the icy thoroughfare. On the far side of the fog-shrouded street was the faint outline of a crown-shaped dome; Hal guessed it belonged to a cathedral.

The boy brought Hal's soup and Hal immediately began to spoon the hot liquid into his mouth. After all of his roaming in the cold, Hal looked different from the previous afternoon when he had arrived in Lithuania.

His fatigue-ridden face jerked up—a fancy red sports car had just pulled over to the curb. Hal gazed at the car, curious; fancy sports cars seemed out of place in this city. The next moment his curiosity gave way to surprise, for out of the driver's side, wearing sunglasses, climbed none other than Jurgita. And she did so with all the grace and loveliness in the world, no more than 15 feet from where Hal sat.

Now she was briskly crossing the street, the collar of her overcoat turned up, concealing her face. And then she entered the cathedral, which was still no more than a faint outline across the way.

When Hal was sure she had gone inside, he put down his spoon, wiped his mouth, and hastened to pay, stealing glance after glance across the street in the direction of the cathedral.

"Is today Sunday?" Hal asked.

"No," snapped the boy with the shaved head.

Leaving a five-*litas* tip, Hal hefted his suitcase and hustled outside. Once across the street, he rushed toward the cathedral. As he drew near he saw that repair work was in progress. But although the cathedral was enveloped in steel scaffolding, it was still in use; old women hooded in black scarves were coming and going to say their prayers. Hal went inside.

The cathedral was much more spacious and ornate than it had appeared from the outside. The interior looked spotless—it must have been recently renovated. Hal's eye was drawn to a series of paintings of biblical scenes, sumptuous murals set between gilded marble pillars. The artwork left Hal with a feeling of majesty, in contrast with the somber mood he had felt outside.

Subdued by this atmosphere of ornate majesty, Hal cautiously took stock of his surroundings. Although few had come to pray, the day not being the Sabbath, Hal's first tentative scan of the interior did not reveal Jurgita. Hal threw caution aside and darted about in search of her. But when he finally did discover her, sitting by herself in prayer, he dared not impose, so absorbed was she in prayer, so pained was her face, so beautiful did she look as she prayed. He waited for her to finish.

When, after a time, she had still not finished, Hal left his suitcase and took another look about. He stared at the murals, the stained-glass windows, and the dome, then returned his gaze toward Jurgita. But she wasn't there! Hal looked about frantically—how could he have missed her? Ah, there she was, scurrying toward the entrance. Hal retrieved his suitcase and took off after her. But by now she was slipping through the door. Hal ran towards it. The few people who were praying looked up and then gazed after the Asian man, rushing through the cathedral with a huge suitcase.

Hal emerged from the cathedral to see Jurgita climb into her red sports car across the street. He called out, but too late—the car had just zoomed away from the curb. All Hal could do was watch from the steps as it made a broad turn on the plaza in front of City Hall and dissolved in the fog.

Hal remained several minutes on the cathedral steps, his face the picture of discouragement, then let his feet take him where they might. He found himself in an alley, and a short time later the sign for Café Mano came into view; the very place where he and Rimas had thawed out the previous night. In he went, wondering if Rimas might be there. As early as it was, there were no customers, only a cute young lady, obviously bored, who put on a fetching smile as she greeted Hal.

Coughing, Hal sat down at the same table he and Rimas had occupied. He looked out the window and saw a high, cinder-block wall. In places the mortar was missing, giving the cinder blocks an emaciated appearance. Against that backdrop the snow was falling.

In barely intelligible English the cute waitress asked Hal what he wanted. *Pálinka*, he said. And when she brought his drink, he asked her name. But this simple question seemed beyond her comprehension, and she kept repeating "*Pálinka! Pálinka!*" before it suddenly dawned on her what Hal was asking, and her answer changed to "Zoja! Zoja!"

"Zoja" Hal said, "I was here late last night—remember?"

Zoja nodded vigorously with a smile that gave Hal no assurance she actually understood. He proceeded nonetheless: "And do you remember my friend who was with me?"

Zoja replied with the same vigorous nod and the same beaming smile, like a wind-up doll. A look of disappointment creased

Hal's face and he swallowed what he was about to say. But then to his surprise, doll-like Zoja spoke up.

"Rimas! Belarus!"

"You know Rimas?" Hal called out in surprise. "My friend from Belarus?"

He was met yet again with the toy nod and smile.

"Zoja!" Hal asked, "Does Rimas come here often?"

"Sometimes."

"But how do you know his name?"

"Music man."

Hal nodded. "If Rimas comes here, will you give him a message? Will you tell him, 'Hal asks you to leave him a message at the Hotel Užupis'?"

With her vigorous nod and her beaming smile Zoja returned to the bar. Half skeptical, Hal followed her with his eyes, then downed his *pálinka*. He rose, took his suitcase in hand, and went to pay.

"Zoja! Be sure to tell Rimas, if he comes here—tell him, 'Your friend Hal from Hun wants you to leave him a message at the Hotel Užupis.'"

One last time Zoja beamed her broad smile and nodded vigorously.

Leaving a 10-*litas* coin for a tip, Hal went out and set off with purpose down the narrow street. Snow was falling. Some fifty yards farther on the alley opened onto a small plaza occupied by an open-air market. Hal browsed the impoverished stalls until he spotted one that sold hats and mufflers. He picked out a Russian fur hat and a heavy muffler—anything that would offer protection against the chill and damp.

Trying on the hat and muffler, he smiled sheepishly—how silly he must look. But the fat woman at the stall didn't laugh. Regarding Hal with utmost seriousness, she barked, "*O-ri-ji-nal!*" Was she speaking Lithuanian? Russian? Polish? Or some other language, maybe even Užupis?

"What language is *o-ri-ji-nal*?" asked Hal.

But the fat woman didn't understand Hal's English and simply repeated "*O-ri-ji-nal! O-ri-ji-nal!*"

Hal paid the woman, and back came his change with yet another "*O-ri-ji-nal!*"

"*O-ri-ji-nal!*" sounded again, but this time Hal recognized the voice. He turned to see silver-haired Vladimir limping toward him behind a pair of gigantic black dogs. A breed of Doberman? They looked fierce with their muzzles of glinting steel.

"Men make hats, but the hat makes the man, as we like to say in Lithuania," said Vladimir as he shook hands with Hal. "It's true—you are a different man with that hat, a dandy-looking bourgeois."

But Hal's immediate concern was the two black dogs, who were busy at his feet, sniffing first at his suitcase, then putting their snouts to his pants, ready to bite and rip. If not for the muzzles, the next second they might be mauling him.

"Well," said Vladimir, "have you managed to locate the Republic of Užupis?"

In his irritation Hal chose to ignore this. "A fine friend you are, coming along with your vicious dogs and cornering me."

Only then did Vladimir rein in the dogs with a commanding shout. The dogs returned at once to their master and meekly settled their hindquarters on the icy surface of the street.

"No worries—the muzzles are quite strong enough."

Hal responded in a pique, "Men always think their dogs won't bite, and husbands always think their wives won't cheat, as we like to say in Užupis."

Vladimir's only response was a slight twitch at the corner of his mouth. Hal sensed his words had touched a nerve.

Vladimir went back on the offensive. "Since you are still here in Lithuania, it seems you haven't yet found Užupis—how much longer will you wander in search of a state that does not exist?"

Hal's face betrayed another surge of anger, but he calmed himself immediately.

"My father told me stories about the Republic of Užupis. One of them was about a man named Shatunovsky, who walked with a limp. I'd never actually met such a man and so I never believed he existed. But now I know he exists, a man named Shatunovsky who walks with a limp. I know his existence is real, even if he's not the Shatunovsky my father knew. And in the same way, I believe in the existence of my fatherland, the Republic of Užupis."

These words brought a laugh from Vladimir along with a grand display of his ivory teeth and his coral-crimson gums.

"You've been looking to make trouble ever since you met me. It is too bad my name has to be Shatunovsky. And that I walk with a limp... Otherwise a well-dressed young gentleman such as yourself would not be searching for some theoretical basis for the existence of the Republic of Užupis; you would not have to wander around this cold country in search of something that does not exist."

Exasperated by Vladimir's cunning, Hal could only say, "It appears that each person has different memories from the next. My father remembered a man named Shatunovsky who walked with a limp, but you don't remember my father. And I have clear memories of the Republic of Užupis, but you and many others say you don't. Perhaps we could say that people can be differentiated on the basis of their memories."

"All right," said Vladimir, calm and collected. "I will take you to the Republic of Užupis if that is what you really want. And I will introduce you to the president." Seeing Hal's dubious expression, he continued: "But I am not going to force you. And even if I do not take you, another of our kind-hearted citizens of Vilnius surely will."

"I don't understand," said Hal.

"Then follow me." So saying, Vladimir limped off after his dogs.

Hal set off behind them, still feeling skeptical.

They had been walking downhill for about five minutes when a narrow river appeared; It was actually a stream, Hal thought. River or stream, there they were, at its edge.

"Here we are—the Vilnia River." Vladimir gestured toward the far side. "And there you are—Užupis. In Lithuanian, *Užupis* means 'on the far side of a river,' see?"

Hal listened silently.

"Look," said Vladimir. "This sign marks the border."

Hal followed Vladimir's extended arm to a sign that was posted where the bridge began; it read, "Entering the Republic of Užupis." He broke into a grin.

"Are you ready?" said Vladimir. "Then follow me."

And off he went across the bridge, Hal in his wake. On the other side Vladimir came to a stop before a café named Užupis.

"I guess you could call this the Republic of Užupis capitol building. Come on in—I will introduce you to some very important people."

Hal followed Vladimir and his canine entourage into the café.

The interior, what Hal could see of it, appeared to be partitioned into several large rooms. Vladimir limped about, black dogs in tow, scanning the rooms. Only a couple of them were occupied. To Hal's surprise—for it was still morning—the men were drinking. Most of them recognized Vladimir and rose to greet him. Vladimir shook hands with each in turn, his voice and expression conveying exaggerated delight. At the same time his eyes flicked about in search of "the very important people."

Finally, after canvassing each of the rooms, Vladimir cried out: "Hey, Your Excellency the Prime Minister!"

At the far side of the last room a man was asleep at a table. Vladimir limped across the room and sat down opposite him. "Tomas! Wake up! A man of Užupis has come from far off to see you!"

This brought the man's head up. At first glance the man appeared to be in his mid-forties, but it was difficult to say for sure because of the black beard that covered his features. The man put his glasses on, then extended a hand in delight. "Hey, Vladimir!"

"Where's the president?" said Vladimir, looking hugely amused as he shook hands with the man called Tomas.

"He went off to Riga. Won't be back for a few days."

They continued to speak in Lithuanian, Vladimir presumably explaining the whys and wherefores of Hal's visit.

Black-bearded Tomas nodded continually as he listened. Finally he rose, and with exaggerated politeness extended his hand. "Be my guest, my good man. May I introduce myself? I am Tomas

Sabaitis, Prime Minister and Minister of Foreign Affairs of the Republic of Užupis, at your service."

Hal found the man a bit ridiculous but managed to suppress a smile as he shook hands.

"My name is Hal."

"Hal?"

"That's right: Hal."

"Well, Mr. Hal, welcome to the Republic of Užupis, a sovereign state." And with that, Tomas produced a ridiculously large business card and presented it to Hal. At the top of the card, where you would expect to see a representation of the national flag, was a logo of an outstretched hand with a hole in the palm. Printed below was "Tomas Sabaitis, Prime Minister of the Republic of Užupis."

So great was the disparity between this grand business card and the man with the black beard who called himself the Prime Minister of the Republic of Užupis that, in spite of himself, Hal burst out laughing.

Tomas accepted this with a look of utter satisfaction. "In the Republic of Užupis everyone has the right to laugh. And that's because everyone has the right to be happy—and the right not to be happy too. Please, will you have a seat?" And when Hal was seated, Tomas produced a flask of vodka from his overcoat, filled a shot glass, and offered it to Hal. "In honor of Mr. Hal."

But Hal demurred.

"Oh?" said Vladimir. "Vodka is a staple in this country. A man who turns down vodka in Užupis will not survive."

"That is right," chimed in Tomas. "Vodka and happiness go hand in hand," as we say in Užupis.

"But Mr. Prime Minister, sir," said Hal, "why aren't you speaking Užupis?"

The question took Tomas by surprise. He fumbled for an answer. "Well, I thought as how maybe you might not understand…"

"But I do understand. I've forgotten how to speak it, but I still understand it when I hear it."

"Good lord," broke in Vladimir. "You mean there is actually an Užupis language?"

"Yes, there is," Hal said as he recalled Urbonas's words the previous evening. "'*Soa ra, Hal?*' Do you know what that means?"

Tomas and Vladimir merely looked at each other, not answering.

"It's Užupis for 'Hal, is that you?' How about '*Chi maerinan Urbonas. Chia ure soari chamaira*'—do you know what that means?"

The other two men remained silent.

"It means 'My name is Urbonas. I knew you would come back.'"

At this, Vladimir's cunning expression gave way to a sudden peal of laughter. "Well, I guess that makes you a true citizen of Užupis, manufacturing a lie like that so quickly. You are surely a genius at lying, pretending you can speak Užupis."

Tomas for his part couldn't have been more delighted. "Yes, that is the guiding belief behind the founding of Užupis: lying is the greatest virtue, as long as you can make people happy. To be true to that guiding belief, we chose April Fool's Day to celebrate the founding of Užupis."

Their frivolous attitude was not to Hal's liking, but he didn't let on.

"Your Excellency, there's something I'd like to ask. When, exactly, was your republic founded, and by whom?"

"Four years ago," said Tomas, "and Romas Lileikis was the driving force. He gathered together the ministers and founded the republic, and he is now our president."

"And on which principles is your country founded?" When Tomas seemed not to understand the significance of this question, Hal added, "Are you aware that the Republic of Užupis has a long history? Just consider how far it used to spread southwest of here—Lithuania, Latvia, Estonia, for starters; Poland, Romania, Belarus, even Ukraine—they were all part of Užupis."

Vladimir clapped once and erupted in laughter.

Tomas blinked a couple of times before responding. "Of course I know that. Užupis was a large country that extended throughout Europe and Russia—it even included China."

This brought another clap and guffaw from Vladimir.

There followed a half hour of conversation between Hal and Tomas. But it never reached a serious plane, for Tomas and Vladimir treated everything Hal said as a joke.

Finally Hal shook hands with Tomas, saying, "Thank you, Your Excellency, for receiving me." And then to Vladimir, in a cynical tone, "I pray you will regain your lost memories." And with that he left the café.

Once again Hal set out on the snowy streets, thinking that in the meantime Rimas might have left a message for him. It wasn't that far back to the hotel. But at the front desk he was told that he had had no visitors, nor was there any message for him.

CHAPTER 7 For the Love of Vilma

Outside the Hotel Užupis Hal crossed a bridge. Feeling hurried but walking aimlessly, he found himself in front of a huge structure that he took for a government building. Just then he remembered what the immigration official at the airport had told him the previous afternoon: if he didn't leave Lithuania within forty-eight hours he was to visit the Ministry of Foreign Affairs and report to the office that dealt with foreign nationals. He managed to find the form he'd been issued, and checked the address—he had arrived at the very place.

The huge door opened onto a vast lobby. Directly before Hal was a staircase. Whom to ask for directions? The few people he saw scurried past him and out of sight. Finally he noticed a uniformed official and asked the way to the office for foreign nationals.

With a troubled look the man explained in Lithuanian, slowly and deliberately, doing his utmost to make himself understood to his foreign visitor. Hal, of course, knew not a word of what the man said, and so he responded, just as slowly and deliberately, but in English, "I wish to see the official who is responsible for foreign nationals."

The uniformed man again did his best to explain. He seemed to understand Hal's English but could not himself answer in that language. And so Hal tried again, this time in French, and then in German. But the result was the same, the official speaking in Lithuanian. Finally Hal tired of the attempt.

The man looked tired as well. Realizing his explanations were futile, he found a piece of paper and wrote a large '3' on it, then pointed up the staircase. Hal made the connection and nodded. With a look of utter satisfaction the man began to chatter away in Lithuanian, then wrote '339' on the paper. Hal produced a satisfied smile of his own and held out his hand to the official. The man shook it while continuing his spiel, then gesticulated animatedly as Hal started up the steps, presumably explaining the location of room 339.

At the third-floor landing Hal faltered before venturing into the left hallway, which was cramped and dim. The wooden floor squawked with every step he took, prompting Hal to tiptoe.

The layout was byzantine—how old was the building anyway? One cramped, dim corridor connected with another, and in some places the ceiling was so low that Hal had to hunch over as he walked. The stochastic arrangement bespoke numerous additions and renovations over the centuries. Hal soon realized that finding room 339 would not be nearly as easy as he had assumed. On he walked, huge suitcase in one hand, scrap of paper in the other, looking down side corridors in both directions, and finally he was lost. He tried to retrace his steps, but this proved difficult. He was in a maze, and there was no one of whom he could ask the way.

Finally Hal came to a bench at one of the turns and he sat his tired body down. As he rested he heard the click of shoe heels against wood, and soon a large, ostentatious man with a grave expression came marching toward him. Should he ask? No. The man looked standoffish, and Hal was savoring the opportunity to rest. The man walked straight toward Hal, then turned down the corridor to the left.

A short time later a couple came into sight. They looked like downhearted farmers, and the man was carrying a large goose. The woman scooted up to Hal and said something. They too seemed to have lost their way in the dark maze of hallways. But Hal understood not a word of what either of them said.

"I'm sorry but I don't speak Lithuanian."

The woman began to plead with him nevertheless; she was on the verge of tears.

"I'm very sorry, but I can't help you," Hal struggled to reply

At this the farmer signaled his wife to stop, whereupon the woman finally realized Hal was not Lithuanian. Distressed, the couple fairly ran down the hall.

Hal rested his head against the wall, feeling spent. He closed his eyes and replayed in his mind the sonata Jurgita had performed at Eigis's the previous night. As he listened to the solemn, dolorous melody, his hands began to move, like a conductor's, in time with the music. Finally, overcome by the passion of the music, he straightened up, his head no longer resting against the wall. Eyes still closed, he followed the melody in his mind. And then he steadied his feet against the floor. Rising resolutely, he strode down the hall, suitcase in hand, and finally spotted a door bearing the number 339.

Hal knocked on the closed door. Back came the resonant voice of a woman, the words Lithuanian. Hal opened the door and saw a bare office, occupied by a single desk. The light coming through the broad window in the facing wall practically blinded him, for his eyes had adjusted to the dim hallways. At the desk slouched a young woman. At Hal's arrival she shot to her feet, delivered from her tedium. She wore a splendid red dress, but the fabric was so thin, more suitable for a summer outing, that it looked incongruous.

"Is this the office for foreign nationals?"

"Yes!" cried the woman in jubilation.

Hal looked about the office, doubtful. How could such an unadorned space be the domain of the Ministry of Foreign Affairs official who was responsible for foreign nationals?

"Sit—sit!" said the woman as she produced a chair for Hal.

What to make of the fidgety woman's grandiloquent friendliness?

"I knew you would come," said the woman once Hal was seated. "I have been waiting for you."

Hal then realized that she was none other than Vilma, from the previous night.

"It's you!" he exclaimed, delighted Vilma had recognized him. "So this is where you work!"

Vilma maneuvered her chair out from behind her desk and pulled it so close to Hal that their knees could have touched. She gave off a mysterious fragrance.

"Where did you stay last night?" she asked.

"At the hotel."

"And have you eaten?"

When Hal merely shrugged, a compassionate look came to Vilma's face and tears gathered in her eyes.

Feeling awkward, Hal hastened to explain the reason for his visit: "I'm here to extend my stay. I was asked to do so by the immigration official at the airport yesterday. I don't have a visa, and she said that if I don't leave within forty-eight hours then I need to apply for an extension." And he handed Vilma the form he had been given at the airport.

"I know," said Vilma as she took the form. "Inga told me about you when she came home from work yesterday. That is why I knew you were coming."

"Who is Inga?"

"My little sister. She is the immigration inspector you met at the airport. She told me that a very handsome Asian gentleman arrived and that he did not have a visa. And that he was going to the Republic of Užupis. And so I went to the hotel last night, expecting I would see you. And I did."

Hal chuckled. Yes, he thought, the uniformed woman did resemble Vilma.

"I knew who you were the instant you arrived at the hotel," Vilma continued in a dreamy tone. "You in your snow-coated hair, with your suitcase ... it was fantasy itself. And your face, the mystique of it!"

Discomfited, Hal attempted to return to the matter at hand. "The extension won't be a problem, will it?"

Vilma was mum, seemingly lost in thought, and then she said, "Well, it's not that simple. There has to be a compelling reason. A natural disaster, for example, or ... marriage to a Lithuanian woman ..." When Hal reacted in astonishment she touched his knees with hers reassuringly. "No need to worry. I will take care of this. Trust me."

Hal was relieved. "One more thing—I want to find out about the Republic of Užupis. And since your area is foreign nationals, perhaps you know something about it?"

Suddenly there was a knock on the door. Vilma jumped to her feet in surprise. She quickly tidied herself, then called out in Lithuanian. Hal took her to be saying, "Come in!"

The door opened and there stood the farm couple with the goose. They inched inside, releasing a torrent of tearful pleas. Vilma snapped at them in irritation. Undeterred, the couple continued their fervid outburst. But Vilma was unyielding. Shouting, she drove them back to the threshold.

The wife stopped there and held out the goose to Vilma, saying, "I *told* you, our daughter Judita ran away. She's only thirteen. We're giving you our goose—won't you *please* find her for us?"

Hal perked up at these words, which were unmistakably Užupis.

It wasn't clear if Vilma had understood, but she held her ground, finally shoving the woman out into the hall with her husband. No sooner had she locked the door than the couple began pounding on it, screaming and pleading. But the clamor soon ceased and there was only the creaking of the wooden floor in the hallways and footsteps receding into the distance. Then all was quiet.

"It is really difficult with these farmers and their missing daughters," Vilma sighed. "They think that if they give me a goose they will get their daughter back."

"There has to be a place they can go for help with their daughters," Hal consoled her.

Vilma, more chipper now, took her place across from Hal.

"You would think so, yes. If they have problems they should go to the Ministry of Agriculture and talk with somebody who deals with farmers. And that ministry is right upstairs. But the farmers in this country are so ignorant—they march into any old office expecting help with finding their runaway daughters. And the result is, we cannot do our work." And then in a fit of aggravation she buried her face in Hal's lap and began to sob.

At his wit's end, Hal looked out the window. Snow was falling gently.

"But Vilma," Hal said, patting her on the back.

Vilma waited, motionless.

"What the wife said at the end... was she speaking Užupis?"

Vilma jerked up and smoothed back her hair. She was once again composed. "Užupis? For heaven's sakes, is there such a language? Those stupid farmers, they still use Russian sometimes."

"But she wasn't speaking Russian—I'm sure of it."

"Well, if it wasn't Russian," Vilma hastened to explain, "either it was a dialect or... yes, it must have been a dialect—in Lithuania some of the farmers have a strange dialect."

Before Hal could respond there came a disembodied voice that carried the weight of authority. "Miss Vilma!"

Once again Vilma shot to her feet. "I'm being summoned," she said theatrically. Picking up the form Hal had left on her desk, she checked herself in the mirror, smoothing back her hair and applying lipstick. Finally she undid the top button of her dress, allowing a better view of her cleavage. Preparations complete, she posed at the door to the next office. Smoothing out her dress one last time, she slipped through the door. Aha, thought Hal, *that's* the Office for Foreign Nationals; he was in the secretary's office.

Hal gazed out the window and grew flustered—the snow had changed to great thick flakes.

A short time later Vilma reappeared. "He will see you now. Please come in."

"Who?" asked Hal.

"The director of the Office for Foreign Nationals."

Hal rose and hefted his suitcase.

Vilma gently fussed with his clothing, hastening to tell him in a soft, secretive voice, "You do not need to talk at length. Lately he has been very irritable—problems at home. So trust me and everything will turn out all right."

The director turned out to be the large, aloof man Hal had seen in the hallway. As Hal followed Vilma into the office, the man rose and with an overblown gesture extended his hand to Hal before launching into a tedious greeting in Lithuanian that to Hal's ears sounded more like a speech. Vilma did her best to interpret. Hal listened and nodded agreeably, offering a brief response in English, which Vilma interpreted. And now the man nodded. Hal found it ludicrous—the head of the Ministry of Foreign Affairs Office for Foreign Nationals needing interpretation to understand the simplest greeting in English.

The man indicated a chair and said something in Lithuanian that Hal assumed to be "Please have a seat." Vilma interpreted for good measure. "Thank you," said Hal as he sat. Vilma made sure to interpret this as well.

Hal took in the office, which was furnished as sparely as Vilma's, save for the luxury of a larger desk and an extra chair.

"The director's name is Mr. Beltran," said Vilma to Hal. Her tone was more formal now. "He speaks no English, and so I will interpret for you. The office head wishes to extend you a warm welcome to our country." So saying, Vilma took a seat beside Hal.

"Thank you for the warm welcome," said Hal to the man. Vilma interpreted. After a contented nod the man replied in Lithuanian. Vilma interpreted.

"The director asks if everything is to your liking here; he asks if you have encountered any inconvenience."

Hal replied that the country was beautiful and that he had encountered no major inconveniences. Vilma promptly interpreted. The director looked even more contented. But what came next was outlandish.

"I offer you my hearty congratulations on your decision to marry my secretary, Miss Vilma Slavikas."

Hal understood perfectly, for the words were Užupis. Surprised though he was, he didn't protest, thinking perhaps he had misheard. And then Vilma interpreted: "He says that if he may say so, you may trust in his interpreter, Miss Vilma Slavikas. Not only is she fluent in English, she is also quite capable as an interpreter."

Here was another surprise for Hal. Had Hal in fact misunderstood the director? Or was Vilma putting on an act to help Hal extend his stay in Lithuania? He recalled Vilma mentioning "a compelling reason": a natural disaster, for example, or marriage to a Lithuanian woman. And so, for the time being, he suppressed his doubts.

"Yes, I agree that Miss Vilma is an excellent interpreter."

After Vilma had interpreted this, the director regarded the two of them, beaming in contentment. "You certainly make a fine couple. Tell me, when and where did you first meet?" This too was spoken in Užupis. Hal found himself in a dilemma, and waited for Vilma to interpret.

"He says you are a splendid young man. He asks what he can do to help you."

Hal was in a fix. Should he respond to the director's question, or to Vilma's interpretation of it? Better to respond to Vilma's interpretation. Because whatever Hal said, Vilma would interpret as she saw fit.

"First of all, I wish to extend my stay in Lithuania. And I would like to ask if you know of the Republic of Užupis. I have reason to believe you know something about that country, because you are speaking Užupis."

Vilma flinched at the mention of Užupis. Was that why she took Hal's hand as she interpreted? The abrupt gesture disconcerted Hal. But the director seemed to find it perfectly natural.

"You say you met at the bar in the Hotel Užupis? Well, that's where I met my wife, Zita. And I never miss one of Eigis's parties. It's great to see all those fun-loving boozers. But last night something came up at home." Again, the words were Užupis.

Vilma interpreted: "You ask me about the Republic of Užupis? Why are you looking for it here in our country? In this country you shouldn't be thinking of another. Is this not a beautiful country? And there are plenty of beautiful women, too. Life is short—don't waste it looking for a country that doesn't exist."

Hal's dilemma continued. As long as Vilma was interpreting as she saw fit, any attempt by Hal to respond to the director would be meaningless. But he pressed on nonetheless. "There's something strange here: whenever I mention the Republic of Užupis, why do people insist that it doesn't exist? Why do some of them treat Užupis as a laughingstock, making up a fake Republic of Užupis complete with a so-called president and prime minister? Do the people here have a complex about the notion of a Republic of Užupis?"

Vilma looked disturbed when she heard this, but the next moment began interpreting in Lithuanian.

"I appreciate your concern," the director responded, "but it's not much of an issue. It's just that my wife can be unpredictable, and it makes life difficult for me. Then again, doesn't every family have such issues? But so much for that. When are you thinking of getting married?"

Vilma interpreted: "I'm sure you have your reasons for being fixated on something called the Republic of Užupis. But my position is simple: I don't believe it exists. And if you can rid yourself of that illusion and settle in this country, our government will offer you assistance—not a large sum, mind you, but enough to help you to enjoy your life here."

By now Hal's head was spinning. He placed a hand on his forehead. As he considered how to respond, Vilma subtly poked him in the side, prompting him to say something.

"What I don't understand," Hal said reluctantly, "is how you are able to speak Užupis. Who could you possibly have learned it from? It must have been your parents. And they must have learned it from *their* parents. Is it possible to speak the language of a country that doesn't exist? Someone is telling a big lie."

Vilma contemplated before interpreting.

The director nodded. "Very good, very good. Congratulations once again on your marriage. Well, the next order of business is for me to issue this beautiful young couple a license for marriage to a foreign national." Procuring the form from a folder, he signed and stamped it.

As he was doing so, Vilma interpreted: "The language I am speaking is not Užupis, it is a dialect spoken in the border area to the northeast. And now that we're finished talking about the Republic of Užupis, all that's left is for me to sign and stamp this form, which grants you an extension to your stay in this country."

The director waited for Vilma to finish, and passed her the form. Then he rose and once again offered Hal his hand. Hal rose briskly in response. The director gave Hal a vigorous handshake, his huge hand covering Hal's, and whispered conspiratorially, "Miss

Vilma has a big bottom, which means she will bear you many children. As the saying goes, a country grows from the bottom up!" He punctuated this comment with a mischievous wink.

Vilma blushed and smiled before interpreting: "Rest assured that your extension is now granted. All the women in this country are beautiful, but you must grab the nearest one. As the saying goes, if you love the one you are with, you will have the country in the palm of your hand."

Toting his suitcase, Hal followed Vilma as she returned to her office. He kept a dismal silence.

Vilma could not have been more buoyant. "You can stay with us starting tonight," she said. "We're as good as married now." So saying, she handed Hal a slip of paper with her address written on it. Bewildered, he pocketed it.

"There are five of us," Vilma explained, "my parents, Inga, her boyfriend Kornelius, and me. And we have three bedrooms, one for my parents, one for Inga and Kornelius, and you and I can use the third one."

Hal was speechless.

"In Lithuania it's common for a daughter to bring home her boyfriend to live with her. So there's nothing to worry about, just come on over, all right?"

Without a word Hal went out into the hall.

Vilma trailed behind, saying, "I wish I could go home with you right now, but I do not get off work until six. I will give you my card. There is my office phone number and there is my home number and there is my cell phone number. Call me around six and I will rush out and meet you, wherever you are."

Hal added the card to the slip of paper in his pocket.

Vilma escorted him to the entrance. That was as far as she went, her flimsy dress offering scant protection against the cold.

"I will be waiting," she said eagerly, her tone poignant.

Hal set out with his suitcase into a snow squall.

CHAPTER 8 At Café Mano

Walking aimlessly, Hal saw, off in the distance, a Russian Orthodox church. The structure, with its dome floating in the snowy void, possessed an otherworldly beauty. Drawn by the sight, Hal proceeded toward it, across the snowy expanse.

Arriving at the church, Hal was surprised to see a red sports car parked along the street. Was it Jurgita's car, the one he had seen from the restaurant near City Hall that morning? If so, then she must be nearby. Hal surveyed the area with renewed interest. But apart from the church, he saw no place she might have gone. But here was her car, patiently awaiting its owner. With this in mind, Hal entered the church.

Unlike the cathedral, the interior of the Russian Orthodox church was arranged in meticulous detail. Every wall held a dizzying profusion of portraits of saints, and every corner and recess was populated with figurines of varying shapes and hues. Hal was reminded of a shaman's shrine he had once seen, replete with flowers, pictures, and talismans. And unlike the solemn majesty he had felt in the cathedral, the mood here was cozy and folksy, and the interior brighter and more opulent.

Quite a few people were at prayer, the majority of them older women, presumably Russian or Lithuanian. But instead of remaining seated in one place while praying, as they would have done in the cathedral, they circulated slowly like pilgrims, paying their respects in turn to the portraits of the saints and to the figurines arrayed throughout the church. But, in spite of their movement, the interior was absolutely quiet.

Hal gazed blankly at the intricate interior and the unanticipated wealth of sights. If Jurgita were here, it would be no easy task finding her. She would likely be slipping among the other visitors, trying to keep out of sight, as she had done that morning in the cathedral. So Hal decided first to make a circuit of the interior. Holding his suitcase, as always, he began his march. Left and right went his head as he inspected the various recesses. How absurd he must have looked, neither a person come to pray nor a well-meaning traveler. And perhaps for this reason, several of the old women shot looks of displeasure at the Asian man for his lack of propriety. Hal took no notice, however, and continued to scour the ins and outs of the sanctuary.

But when, at the end of his circuit, he had failed to spot Jurgita, he became morose. After all, why would someone who had prayed at the cathedral that very morning come here to pray all over again? At this thought, a fresh wave of despondency washed over him.

Hal rushed outside—perhaps Jurgita had stolen out while he was making his rounds. But there was the red sports car, the snow accumulating on it. Relieved, Hal reentered the church and began another slow circuit. Once again there was no sight of Jurgita. Exhausted, Hal slumped into a chair. On the wall before him was a scroll containing a portrait of a church elder with eagle eyes and a bushy red beard. Hal gaped at the portrait with its comic, exaggerated features and then, whether in prayer or in response to his fatigue, went down on bended knee and leaned over. There he remained, motionless, the figure with the eagle eyes and the bushy red beard appearing to bend over to regard him.

Perhaps three minutes had passed when Hal suddenly straightened up. The instant he did so he spied Jurgita in a far recess, deftly crossing herself before a portrait of a saint. Her golden hair was concealed by a dark scarf, but even at this distance her grief-stricken eyes and forehead, and the haughty bridge of her nose were unmistakable. Hal shot to his feet and grabbed his suitcase. But the next moment she was gone. Hal rushed to the far side of the sanctuary, to where he had seen her, but the only person there was a fat old woman kneeling in prayer. Hal looked about, glassy-eyed, and there in a different recess was Jurgita, making the sign of the cross with the same deft motion, a nimble, delicate movement, not unlike that of a chicken pecking at feed. And then she was out of sight once again, with Hal in hot pursuit.

He arrived at the next recess and there she was, hands clasped together and praying before a portrait of another saint. Finally—she was right in front of him, motionless.

"Jurgita!"

"Ssh," she whispered, a finger to her lips. And then she turned back to the portrait, lowered her head reverently, and resumed praying. Hal regarded her vacantly.

Finally she finished her prayer and made the sign of the cross. As she moved to the next portrait she spoke quickly to Hal in a soft, secretive tone: "I'm praying for you. I'm praying that you find the Republic of Užupis safely."

"Thank you."

"My husband went looking for the Republic of Užupis too, and he died," Jurgita whispered as she lit a stick of incense.

Taken aback, Hal listened silently.

"They say he killed himself, but I don't believe it. There's no doubt in my mind he was murdered." A tinge of sadness came briefly to her face, but she managed to suppress it as she made the sign of the cross.

"Would you tell me what you know about the Republic of Užupis?" said Hal.

Intent on her prayers, Jurgita didn't immediately respond. "I can't now," she whispered. "Tonight at nine, meet me at Café Mano."

"Café Mano?"

"Oh, I forgot—you don't know where it is."

"Well, I was there last night with Rimas, my friend from Belarus, and I happened upon it again this morning, but I'm still not sure I could find my way there."

Jurgita considered this for a moment. "Do you have pen and paper? I'll write down the address."

Hal quickly produced his address book and fountain pen. She took the pen in her left hand and the address book in her right, cast a cautious glance about her, and wrote in a flash. So, she was left-handed. Hal recalled that it was with the finger of her left hand that she had shushed him just now.

After she had finished, Jurgita regarded the pen in amazement. "A Mont Blanc—a really old one too."

"Yes. It belonged to my late father."

"Well, my husband had one exactly like it. And it was left to him by *his* late father," said Jurgita as she returned the pen and address book to Hal. "Here's the address. It's not that far from Eigis's. Well, so long for now. I'll see you tonight at nine."

Hal nodded, then hefted his suitcase.

Hal made straight for the Hotel Užupis. There was ample time until nine o'clock, and the first thing to do was check if anyone had left a message for him. But at the hotel there was only the message he had left for Rimas that morning.

Hal obtained a sheet of paper and took a seat in the lounge. At this early hour few people were there. He began to compose a second message to Rimas:

> *My dear friend Rimas,*
>
> *The message I left for you this morning is still here, and there is no reply from you. Presumably you are on a bus for Kishinev at this time, since the snow we had last night didn't develop into a heavy snowfall today.*
>
> *Assuming you are settled on your bus, there is a good chance you will never read this letter. (Granted, if you come to Vilnius around this time next year to see Vilma, and you happen to drop by the Hotel Užupis, then this letter might come into your hands. But I don't think I will remain in Vilnius until then. I will leave here within a day, for I must return to my homeland of Užupis.)*
>
> *I am writing this letter for two reasons, even though I realize you may never read it. First of all, I haven't given up on the possibility that you may still be in Vilnius. And second, if in fact you are staying, then I hope we might meet once again.*
>
> *But in spite of my hopes and expectations, the fact is that you are most likely traveling along an endless, snow-covered road*

on a bus for Kishinev. Even so, you can be sure I will keep the promise I made to you last night, and that by doing so we will avoid any misunderstanding on that issue in the future.

You may be wondering why I bring this up just now. The reason is that today I was issued a marriage license with which to marry Miss Vilma. On the surface this may appear to be a complete breach of my trust with you, and accordingly, grounds for a serious misunderstanding on your part. But once you know the details there will be absolutely no misunderstanding.

This afternoon I visited the Ministry of Foreign Affairs Office for Foreign Nationals—the reason being that if I remain in Lithuania longer than forty-eight hours, I'm required to obtain an extension. But, unexpectedly, I met Vilma; I didn't realize she worked there.

I was told that, barring special circumstances, such as a natural disaster or marriage to a Lithuanian woman, an extension would not be easy to obtain. And so to help me Vilma arranged for me to obtain a marriage license with which to marry her. I believe that Miss Vilma's helping a foreigner like myself, who had nowhere else to turn, is proof of her noble and benevolent disposition.

And I am sure you realize that there is a vast difference between a marriage license and an engagement contract. The marriage license I received means only that I can marry Vilma, not that I will marry her. And in fact I have absolutely no intention of marrying her. I hope you will have not a shred of doubt about this matter.

Last, I would like to hear more of the story you told me last night at Eigis's party about the Republic of Užupis. If you are still in Vilnius, I would be truly grateful if you could continue that story. And if you have remained in Vilnius but do not have time to meet, then it would be good if you could write down for me all that you know about the Republic of Užupis.

6:28 p.m.
Your faithful friend Hal

Hal read over the letter, then folded it and left it with the man at the front desk before leaving.

Outside the hotel it was already dark. There was still plenty of time before nine o'clock, but Hal moved quickly nevertheless, allowing for the possibility that he might get lost.

But he found Café Mano without incident. A new shift had begun, and at the bar, in place of cute Zoja, was a tall, blonde-haired young man. Hal settled himself at the table where he and Rimas had sat the previous night, and the young waiter came to take his order. Hal asked about Zoja and was told she had left for the day. Had a Belarus musician named Rimas dropped by? asked Hal. The young man shrugged and said he didn't know a man by that name. With a sigh Hal ordered a *pálinka*. He looked out through the window and saw snow falling against the backdrop of the gloomy brick wall that had lost its cement.

Just then a dainty young lady and a man of similar age who must have been six and a half feet tall entered the café, removed their coats, and brushed the snow from their hair. The woman spotted Hal and came over, beaming from ear to ear.

"Hello, Mr. Hal!" she said, extending a hand.

Hal shook hands with her, wondering who she could possibly be.

"I'm Inga," said the lady.

"Inga?"

"Vilma's sister, Inga."

Finally Hal made the connection—she was the woman in the olive-green uniform who had inspected his passport the previous afternoon. Out of her uniform she looked like a different person.

"Aha—the woman who was going to deport me because I didn't have a visa," Hal jested.

"That wouldn't have made Vilma very happy," responded Inga in kind. And then she introduced her tall companion: "This is Kornelius—my boyfriend."

"Hi!" said Kornelius as he stuck out his hand. To Hal the hand seemed as large as Kornelius was tall. More striking were the young man's features: there was something Asian about them.

"Hi!" said Hal, shaking hands with him.

"I have something to talk with you about," said Inga. "Do you mind if we join you—just for a little while?"

Sensing the importance of what Inga had to say, Hal obliged, though he didn't particularly relish the prospect. The couple took seats across the table from him.

"When my sister came home she told us you would be coming to live with us today—is that true?" When Hal merely shrugged, Inga's face took on a look of concern. "Needless to say, none of us has the right to oppose your coming to live with us—in this country it is the daughter's right to bring her boyfriend home with her. There is a problem, though." When Hal remained silent, Inga hastened to add, "But do not get me wrong. We would welcome a gentleman like you into our family, all of us. It is just that my parents' apartment is too cramped for six people—it is public housing, built back when we were part of Russia. There are three bedrooms, but the one Vilma uses is not much bigger than a closet, and it is not heated—it is not really suitable for a gentleman like yourself."

Hal finally spoke up: "I don't think there's any cause for concern. I have no plans to marry Miss Vilma."

"Oh, look what I have done," said Inga, crestfallen. "I have created a big misunderstanding. Please, do not get me wrong. I have no objection to your moving in with us—and I would have no right to, even if I did. I merely wanted to tell you in advance about our situation, so you will not be disappointed. And so I beg of you, please do not be angry and please do not go to extremes, saying you will not marry Vilma. If you would like, we can switch rooms with you. I will gladly offer our room to the two of you. It is as tiny as Vilma's but at least the heating has not entirely broken down yet."

"No, it is *I* who must beg *you* not to misunderstand *me*," Hal managed to reply. "When I say I have no plans to marry Vilma, it's not because of the small room, or because it's not heated. And Vilma is obviously a beautiful and affectionate lady who would make any man happy. But I cannot marry her. Because I must leave this country, perhaps as soon as tomorrow. And there's another reason—a friend of mine from Belarus loves Vilma a hundred, no, a million times more than I do, and I made a promise to him last night, right here at this table. I promised him I would not marry Vilma."

"But if you have no plans to marry Vilma, why then did you go to the Ministry of Foreign Affairs Office for Foreign Nationals to get a marriage license?"

"That wasn't the document I went there for. I went to that office to extend my stay here, that's all. You told me, remember? That if I stayed in this country more than forty-eight hours I would have to visit the Ministry of Foreign Affairs Office. I realize it hasn't been forty-eight hours yet, but I thought there was a good chance I would stay longer."

Inga listened patiently, and Hal continued: "But Miss Vilma told me it's not easy to get an extension unless something like a natural disaster or marriage to a Lithuanian woman is involved. And so I think she arranged for the marriage license as a way to help me get the extension."

"Good heavens!" said Inga in consternation. And after a pause: "Marrying a Lithuanian woman to get an extension? I've never heard of such nonsense. You must think she is so forward— please forgive her, she wasn't acting out of malice. You can understand that, can't you?" She briefly fell silent, sadness filling her face. "This kind of thing happened before. Vilma fell in love with another foreign gentleman who came to Lithuania wanting to visit the Republic of Užupis. He was the mirror image of you. But it never blossomed: the man never reciprocated."

"What happened to him?" Hal practically shouted, so surprised was he.

A troubled look came to Inga's face, and she didn't immediately answer. "When I saw you at the airport yesterday I was thunderstruck—you looked so much like that other man. And you too said you were going to the Republic of Užupis. So as soon as I got home from work I told Vilma."

"But what happened to the *man*?"

"He died," Inga finally replied. "Shot himself, in a vacant apartment here in Vilnius."

"And why did he do that?"

"That's what we don't know."

A brief silence settled over them. And then Kornelius, perhaps out of boredom, began mimicking a basketball player shooting baskets. At first he used only his hands, but gradually he became more animated, until he was jittering from side to side and pretending to dribble.

"Kornelius!" Inga barked, bringing him to a stop. And then she turned back to Hal. "I am very sorry. Kornelius doesn't understand a word of English, and I am sure he is bored. Please forgive him."

"I don't mind," said Hal. "He's a young man with a young man's energy—can't sit still for a minute."

Inga formed a poignant smile. "It is good that you understand. Kornelius is in fact a basketball player. We have quite a few tall people in our country, and they make the best basketball players in the world. Many of our players have been drafted by professional teams overseas. And most of them make good money. Kornelius is not one of the top players, but even so, he makes a fortune. And so my parents are very proud of me."

"As well they should be. I think any parents would be proud to have a daughter like you—young, pretty, and intelligent."

Inga blushed. "Well," she said sheepishly, "there are plenty of young, pretty, and intelligent daughters. But the reason my parents are proud of me is that Kornelius makes a lot of money." But then her face took on a sad look. "To tell you the truth, though, he is a bit of a simpleton. He is a big man but he acts just like a child. I think it is because he never learned to speak properly when *he* was a child. The language he learned from his father, Urbonas, was a strange one, and he grew up not knowing much Lithuanian, Russian, or Polish. And so he never really learned *anything* properly. Except basketball."

Hal, once again startled, broke in: "Could it have been Užupis that his father taught him?"

At the mention of Užupis, Kornelius jerked his head in Hal's direction. Inga, unaware of Kornelius's reflex reaction, responded to

Hal: "I do not know. What I do know is that Urbonas was a poet, he had a political problem, and he spent a long time in a Siberian labor camp. I hear he was only recently released."

It was only then that Hal noticed the resemblance between Kornelius and the Urbonas he'd encountered the previous evening. An exclamation escaped him. "I'd like to meet Urbonas," said Hal, elation in his voice. "Where could I find him?"

Inga watched Hal in puzzlement, then said something in Lithuanian to Kornelius. After a brief exchange, Inga turned back to Hal, speaking again in English.

"He says you cannot see him. He thinks his father might have died a long time ago in the labor camp."

Hal was dubious. "Didn't you say just now that Urbonas was recently released?"

"Yes, I did. From time to time we hear people say they have seen him—always standing on a street corner at night beneath the falling snow. But the fact is, we have no solid proof that he has returned. If he has, then he would have come looking for Kornelius by now, right?"

Tears welled in Hal's eyes as he heard this.

"Now why did I have to say that?" said Inga, flustered at the sight of Hal. She signaled Kornelius with her eyes—it was time to go. Kornelius rose and extended his hand. Hal shook it, wiping away his tears with his free hand. Again he noticed how large the tall young man's hand was. And there was no mistaking it—Kornelius did look Asian. Farewells concluded, Inga and Kornelius took their leave of Hal.

CHAPTER 9 Jurgita's Husband

Nine o'clock arrived, but not Jurgita. Instead Hal saw, coming through the door of Café Mano, a large farmer clutching a huge goose to his chest—the same middle-aged man Hal had glimpsed outside the airport the previous afternoon.

The farmer looked about, spotted Hal, and approached. *He's brought a message from Jurgita*, Hal decided. The man made certain it was Hal, then said something to him, whether in Lithuanian, Russian, or Polish, Hal couldn't tell. But he thought he heard Jurgita's name. *Are you waiting for Jurgita?*—that was what the man must be saying. When Hal nodded, the man handed him a folded sheet of paper and spoke again. Without waiting for an answer, he rushed off, moving surprisingly quickly for a big man. The man's attire, not to mention the goose, seemed out of place in the cafe, but, to Hal's surprise, none of the others had taken particular notice of him.

Hal unfolded the note. He recognized the writing as Jurgita's. The message read simply, "Please come now to the following address." Below was an address and a sketch map. Hal quickly donned coat, muffler, and hat, paid for his *pálinka*, and stepped outside, suitcase in hand. The air was frigid.

Hal set off downhill on a dark, slippery street, turned left, and walked some two hundred yards. Stopping beneath a streetlight, he checked Jurgita's map. He turned right, into a dark alley. Another two hundred yards farther along, he stopped again and looked about. It was then that Jurgita appeared from the shadows.

"Don't say anything, just follow me," she said, a finger to her lips, before Hal could greet her. "Someone might see us." Off she went around a corner and down another alley. Hal followed, and some twenty yards away they entered a square courtyard surrounded by woebegone four-story buildings.

"This was a ghetto for the Jews before the war," Jurgita whispered as she led Hal through the dismal entrance to one of the buildings. "During the war they were all taken away."

The interior was lit by dim, incandescent bulbs. The building was dilapidated and obsolete, and reminded Hal of an abandoned storehouse. In front of them was the door to an apartment, to the right a staircase.

"This way," whispered Jurgita as she set off up the stairs.

Hal followed, wondering if the structure was typical of apartment construction in the older part of Vilnius. The farther up they went, the worse the condition of the building. The plaster had come off in places, exposing the bare brick within, and elsewhere timbers were shoring up the disintegrating walls. Everywhere it was drafty. On each floor they could hear the faint sounds of television programs and the voices of the residents. Still, it was difficult for Hal to accept that people actually lived in such a squalid building.

At the fourth floor Jurgita finally came to a stop. Hal looked about, amazed.

"It's really run-down, isn't it?" said Jurgita. "But believe it or not, whether you own or rent, these are the most expensive apartments in Vilnius. And every year they get more expensive. Because of the location and because the heating is reliable. Not even professors and staff members in the presidential palace can afford to live here anymore."

Passing her hand along the wall, she removed a loose brick; secreted behind it was the key to her apartment. At the door, she stamped her feet on the mat to remove the snow from her shoes.

"Please come in," she said from inside, where she stamped on a rug at the threshold for good measure. Hal followed Jurgita's example, stamping on the mat outside and scuffing the soles of his shoes on the rug inside.

The interior was dark. Hal couldn't see the layout, but sensed that the apartment was capacious. They seemed to be in a large living room with a bare wood floor, in the middle of which sat a solid, heavy-looking table. Set into the far wall was a large cavity that appeared to be a fireplace.

"I wanted to meet you at Café Mano, but I decided it was too risky. That's why I brought you here. Besides, I wanted to show you some of my late husband's belongings—they're connected with the Republic of Užupis, and since you're going there, I thought they might be of some interest to you."

As she spoke, Hal removed his coat and hat and she disappeared into the gloom to hang them up. Hal lingered in the dark living room, coughing.

"You sound like you've caught a cold. Please, sit," said Jurgita as she reappeared.

Hal took a seat at the table.

Once he was settled, Jurgita spread a tablecloth and placed a soup bowl and spoon before him. "I'll be right back," she said, disappearing again. Presently she came back with a pot of soup. "Here you are! Hot soup is just what you need for your cough." And she ladled the steaming liquid into the bowl.

"Thank you." Hal was exhausted and he tucked into his soup with the alacrity of a starving man. Jurgita stood beside him, looking on approvingly as he slurped the soup, unmindful of all else. He looked up at her. "I really think I have never tasted soup this good in all my life. What is it exactly?"

"Vegetable fish soup. It's traditional Užupis fare—the Lithuanians don't know how to make it."

"Is it just me, or is there jasmine in it? You didn't add a flower to it, did you?"

This brought a delighted giggle from Jurgita—Hal found it scintillating.

"Adding flowers to soup—now there's a marvelous recipe! No, it's not a flower you smell, it's a mushroom. Several varieties grow in the woods here. I like to add a few chunks to the soup—they can help clear a cough." She scooped more soup into Hal's bowl, then took a large loaf of bread from the basket on the table and sliced it for Hal, who by now was no longer coughing.

"It's strange—I feel like I've eaten this soup with the jasmine scent before. But I couldn't tell you where or when." Hal slurped more soup and bit into a slice of bread. Jurgita looked on approvingly.

Suddenly Hal looked up, his gaze fastening onto the wall opposite. His eyes had finally adjusted to the dimly lit interior, and there on the wall above the fireplace was mounted a flag.

"Isn't that the Užupis flag?" Hal asked, enchanted at the sight.

"Yes," said Jurgita with a wistful smile. "It was left to me when my husband died."

Hal approached the fireplace in a trance and gazed in rapture at the flag.

"You're an Užupis man for sure if you recognize the flag." And then, lost in nostalgia, Jurgita began murmuring. "Whenever I see it I think of a scene from my childhood. I couldn't have been any older than five, and I really didn't know what it was all about, but I remember a lot of people out in the street waving that flag and calling out to someone, welcoming him. Oh, now it's coming back—it was a parade and there were cars. There was a great man—he wore a laurel wreath and he was waving at everybody. He was in a car and the car was moving toward me very slowly. Then the car stopped and the man got out. And he walked up to me and the grownups pushed me toward him and I gave him a bouquet. Everyone clapped, and the man rubbed my cheek and gave me a kiss, and then removed a huge flag that was draped over his shoulders and wrapped it around me. But when he kissed me his beard felt so prickly I almost burst out crying."

"I think I know who you're talking about," said Hal. "It might have been the Užupis man who won the Olympic marathon. I was out on that street too, waving my flag with everyone else when he came back—I can see it now."

"My goodness, so we were both there at that historic moment," said Jurgita, her voice quivering with emotion. "Except that while you were rejoicing, I was on the verge of tears because of that man's beard."

But Hal wasn't really listening, so caught up was he in the excitement of that day from the past. "It really was amazing," he exulted. "The parade went all the way to the presidential palace, and I was standing with my friends where the bridge to the palace begins." To give Jurgita a better idea of where he had stood that day, he took from his pocket the postcard of the ancient castle surrounded by the lake, from the steeple of which flew the very same flag that was mounted on the wall of Jurgita's apartment, the grand castle built with marble, rising against the backdrop of a snow-covered alpine range—the postcard he had shown to Jonas the taxi driver, to Alvydas, and to others besides. "I was standing right here. He passed directly in front of us and went across the bridge—he received a hero's welcome from our Excellency. If you were the girl who presented him with the bouquet that day, then you must have been in the palace courtyard—right around here," Hal said, indicating the area.

Jurgita took the postcard and examined it, oblivious to all else. Closing her eyes, she clutched it to her chest, a long-forgotten strand of memory reviving within her. It was several minutes before she released the postcard from her chest and gazed at it again.

"That's right," she said to herself. "My father crossed that bridge when he left. He was riding a horse, flanked by his men. A great crowd, including his Excellency, were waving goodbye to the procession."

When Hal saw the tears filling Jurgita's eyes his excitement finally abated. He wondered what she would say next.

"This is my father," Jurgita continued, indicating one of several framed photographs mounted on the wall. "He was a general in the Užupis army."

In the photo stood a man in uniform with medals pinned to his chest and two stars on his epaulets. He was a handsome man in his mid-forties with chiseled features, and he struck a grand pose.

"Jurgita, I can see quite a resemblance," said Hal.

"But I'm afraid I don't have many memories of him," said Jurgita with a melancholy smile. "He was killed a long time ago, in the war. In fact that day he crossed the bridge is about the only thing I remember. He never did come back across it."

Hal heaved a great sigh. "I'm so sorry," he said in a grieving tone.

But the next moment Jurgita brightened. "And this is a photo of me and my cousin when I was young." She indicated a framed black-and-white photo, no larger than a cigarette pack. It showed a short, blond-haired girl, who couldn't have been more than five, standing beside a lanky teenage boy. The girl wore a dress and a white bonnet; the boy was dressed in shorts and held a wide-brimmed hat. Hal guessed the photo had been taken at a summer resort. The girl was squinting while the boy looked straight ahead, impassive, the girl's hand in his. What caught Hal's attention was the boy's Asian features.

"Don't I look funny?" said Jurgita. "I'm told we were at Gruzia, on the Black Sea, when it was taken. I don't even remember being there."

"Hmm, your cousin looks Asian," said Hal as he studied the photograph.

"Yes, he does. In other countries we probably wouldn't be called cousins. But in Užupis that's how we were regarded. It's because my father and his father were such close friends—they were like brothers. And so the children of such close friends are called cousins. But it's not a term that's used loosely; we really are considered cousins. And in Užupis," she said, indicating herself in the photo, "girls often marry such cousins. And when they do, they're considered the most blessed of brides, and are held in high esteem by society. If you don't have such a cousin, or if you do, but marry someone else, then you're considered unfortunate. The worst case is if you have such a cousin but don't marry him, and end up marrying a widower with a couple of children—the reason being, it's as if you're divorced from that cousin and you have no other choice. That this long-legged boy came from far, far away to marry this little runt of a girl is proof that we were considered legitimate cousins." And then she lapsed into a sorrowful murmur: "It's because of this cousin that I still have such heartache."

Hal kept a respectful silence, and soon Jurgita, through sheer will power, recovered her cheerfulness: "And look! Here we are on our wedding day," she said, indicating the third of the framed photographs, in which Jurgita in her wedding gown, beaming radiantly, stood next to her husband. The husband resembled Hal, but Hal failed to notice this.

"You're beautiful," said Hal in admiration, "and your husband is good-looking."

"Thank you. We really were happy," said Jurgita in a dreamy

voice. "But not for long." She pointed to a fourth framed photograph. "And that's his family." Centered in the old black-and-white photo was a middle-aged man in full dress uniform, sitting stiff and stern, a medal pinned to his chest. Next to him sat a woman whose clothing bespoke refinement. Standing in front of the man and woman were a little girl and a tall boy who looked a couple of years older. And behind the middle-aged man and the woman was a thirtyish man, tall and with a stylish mustache, striking a pose for the camera. Judging from their dress and the elegant background, they appeared to be a dignitary and his family at the turn of the twentieth century. That this photo was identical to the photo Hal had shown Alvydas and Vladimir the previous night also escaped Hal.

Jurgita commented on the individuals in the photo: "This was my father-in-law; he was an Užupis ambassador, and he ended up posted in some far-off country. And she was my mother-in-law. That pretty little girl was my sister-in-law, and the tall boy was the 'cousin' I ended up marrying. He's really cute, isn't he? And the fashionable gentleman with the mustache was my uncle through marriage—he was a kind of poet laureate of the Užupis people. His name was Urbonas."

"That's Urbonas?" Hal called out in astonishment.

Instead of responding, Jurgita continued her explanation: "They look happy, don't they? Well, they didn't end up happy. They left for some far-off country where the father was the Užupis ambassador. And while they were there, they lost their own country. And without a country to return to, they were in effect exiles."

"Good heavens!" said Hal.

"It was too much for them—their homesickness, I mean," said Jurgita. "My father-in-law died by his own hand—he shot himself."

"Oh no!"

"Homesickness is supposed to be a killer of the Užupis people—it's in their blood. Some people say it's endemic to Užupis. And some say it comes from the Užupis custom of marriage between cousins. When my husband died, I had to get away, so I went to Denmark. But I missed home so much, I had to come back. I returned just yesterday—here to Lithuania, the closest I could get to Užupis. Can you imagine how my father-in-law felt when he wasn't able to return to his homeland?"

Hal nodded. "Something like that happened in Han, where we lived. Han was a kingdom until early in this century, when it was colonized by Ahab. There was an international peace conference in St. Petersburg, and, unknown to Ahab, the king of Han sent an envoy named Chang to let the world know about the suffering of the people of Han at the hands of Ahab. But Chang's plans ran up against obstacles right from the start. Ahab orchestrated the proceedings so that Chang was prevented from appearing before the assembly. Instead he staged a daily protest at the entrance to the assembly building. Several of the St. Petersburg newspapers carried the story of this solitary man and his fervent loyalty, but the world at large wasn't interested. And then one day he was found dead in his shoddy hotel room—the cause of death was never determined."

"I wonder if my husband died like that," said Jurgita. And suddenly she broke down, covering her face.

"I'm sorry, I shouldn't have said that," said Hal, choking up.

With an effort Jurgita brought her emotions under control and looked up. "I'm the one who should apologize. I don't know why I'm acting this way—I guess it comes from meeting someone from Užupis." She continued her story: "And my mother-in-law—she couldn't have been a better wife to him—after he died she lived out the rest of her days in that far-off country, in a home for the insane. That left the pretty little girl an orphan, and she came down with tuberculosis and died at the age of fifteen. So the boy was the only one to hear the news when Užupis regained its independence, and when he came back we got married."

"And what happened to this gentleman?" asked Hal, indicating the man with the mustache, Jurgita's uncle.

"He stayed behind in Užupis—he didn't go with his brother," Jurgita said with a sigh. "He wrote lyric poetry, little gems of poems that earned him the title Poet of the People. But soon Užupis was taken over and he turned to writing resistance poems. That got him taken off to a labor camp in Siberia, and no one has heard of him since."

Hal kept a thoughtful silence before asking, "Did this gentleman happen to have a son named Kornelius?"

"That I don't know," said Jurgita. "But they say he was a skirt chaser, and I wouldn't be surprised if he had a lot of children. What's more, after he was taken away, all the young maidens who adored him, if they had babies they would claim the father was Urbonas. But no one knows if any of that is true."

Hal chuckled.

"Oh—I almost forgot. I was going to show you my husband's things." Jurgita retrieved a squat box from the display cabinet next to the fireplace, then turned on a lamp nearby. "My husband's father—my father-in-law, I mean—received this from the President of the Republic of Užupis." She opened the box to reveal a medal.

"That's a fancy-looking medal," said Hal, unaware he had shown Vladimir the very same medal the previous night. Hal's gaze remained fixed on the medal until he spotted a tiny photograph hidden in a corner of the box. "What's this?" he asked. The black-and-white photo showed a blond-haired girl playing a grand piano, and it bore a similarity to one of the photos Hal had shown Vladimir at Eigis's party. If there was a difference, it was the lady in this photo, who was looking down at the girl with palpable pride. This lady was identical to the woman in the family photograph that Jurgita had just shown Hal.

"Aha!" cried Jurgita in delight. "I was wondering where that photo went."

Hal, however, was perplexed.

"I'm so thankful you found this for me. This was when I was taking piano lessons. And that's the lady who became my mother-in-law. She was my piano teacher."

Baffled, Hal continued to examine the photo. "Strange—I think I've seen that room before—where is it?"

Jurgita giggled, the clarity and loveliness of her voice unchanged. "As well you should—it's the very same room where I was playing the piano last night—at Eigis's."

This drew a look of amazement from Hal.

"That's right," said Jurgita as she observed Hal. "The house where you went last night—Eigis's house—is where my cousin and his family used to live."

Hal nodded. Finally it was all starting to make sense. "Yes, Alvydas told me—he said that a family of noble descent lived there before the colonial period. And now I can see that your husband was the heir to that family."

"Yes, he was," said Jurgita. From the display cabinet she took a revolver. "And this is one of the proud possessions of that noble family," she said cynically. "It made possible the final act of glory of the heir to that family. They tell me it was discovered next to his body. The police said he used it on himself. I don't believe it." Jurgita, mournful, said no more.

Hal regarded her with pity. A heavy silence descended upon them.

Minutes passed and then Jurgita, in an effort to dispel the gloom, forced a sparkling smile and put the muzzle of the revolver to her temple. She used her left hand, making the gesture somehow clumsy and playful.

"I didn't know you were left-handed," said Hal.

The arm holding the revolver fell limply to Jurgita's side. "That reminds me of the Užupis folk belief that left-handed women are widowed early. Well, you're right—I'm left-handed and I was widowed early."

Realizing his callous remark had hurt her feelings, Hal hastened to add, "My mother was left-handed too."

As if she had just remembered something, Jurgita returned to the cabinet and found a slim volume of poetry. "Do you know the Užupis language?" she asked Hal.

"I can understand it but I can't speak it. I guess it's been too long."

"How curious—you sound just like my husband. Well, I'd like to read you a poem—it's called 'Poets of a Colonized Land.'" Leafing through the book with her left hand, she found the poem and began to read in Užupis:

Left-handed are the poets of a colonized land.
Left-handed they eat
Left–handed they drink
Left-handed they love
Left-handed they masturbate.
But their watches, of course, they wear on the right.

The lovemaking of the left-handed poets lacks completion
Leaving all of their daughters mute
Singing silent songs
Crying soundless tears.
But their watches, of course, they wear on the right.

The lovemaking of the mute daughters lacks completion
Leaving all of their husbands blind
Whispering into the night's ears
Sleeping in the night's bosom.
But their watches, of course, they wear on the right.

Left-handed are the poets of colonized lands everywhere
Left-handed they write their poems
Left-handed they nurture their mute daughters
Left-handed they greet their blind sons-in-law.
But their watches, of course, they wear on the right.

Hal, lost in thought during the recitation, heaved a sigh. "What a sad poem—it's terrifying. Gloomy is the fate of a people who have lost their country."

"Yes," said Jurgita. "Urbonas, Poet of the People of the Republic of Užupis during the colonial period, wrote this poem to mourn the passing of the Ukrainian poet Yorslav. Yorslav suffered a similar fate—he was implicated in a plot, and assassinated."

Hal nodded morosely.

"The poem drew tears from many Ukrainians during the colonial period. And it lit the fires of the Ukrainian independence movement."

Hal nodded again, keeping a gloomy silence.

"This is the man who wrote this poem that drew tears from the Ukrainians." So saying, Jurgita indicated a photograph at the front of the book. It was of an Asian man with a stylish mustache, shown from the waist up. He looked to be in the prime of his life. Just looking at the delicate outline of his mouth, people might well take him for a Casanova. It must have been an old photo, and the reproduction was poor, the image bearing streaks.

Hal glumly inspected the photo and once again a heavy silence fell over them.

Finding the silence oppressive, Jurgita went to the window and cautiously opened the curtain. Outside the snow was falling in large flakes. She watched as they fell to the ground, then whirled back to Hal. "We need music." She scurried to the cabinet, pulled out a record, and set it on the turntable of an ancient phonograph. Static hissed from the speakers, followed by music—a solemn and sorrowful prelude.

Hal's head jerked up. The poignant prelude came to an end, and a tenor voice that managed to be both resonant and articulate began to sing the Užupis national anthem. Hal closed his eyes and grew rigid, overcome with fervor.

"Do you know it?" whispered Jurgita. Hal didn't answer. The song reverberated like the boom of fierce waves crashing onto shore. But the next moment the tenor's voice subsided to a gentle whisper, like a breath of breeze on a calm lake.

Hal took advantage of the quiet interval to put his mouth to Jurgita's ear: "You were playing it last night—our national anthem."

"Yes!" Jurgita replied, her voice subdued as well. "Our fatherland!"

The music began to crest once more, and Hal, surrendering to his emotions, took Jurgita in his arms and kissed her with abandon. Jurgita responded with equal intensity, hands clasped about Hal's neck. The tenor's song continued, solemn and gloomy.

Jurgita, gasping for breath, pushed Hal away. "No, I can't. My loving husband and I were in this very room."

"Oh, I'm sorry," panted Hal.

They kept a restless silence as the music's fury peaked, and finally Jurgita opened her arms wide and embraced Hal about the neck, saying, "My poor fellow countryman!" And then she murmured, "My husband would surely forgive me—if only he knew that a lonely wanderer has come in search of Užupis."

Desperately Hal undid her dress. He found her breasts and began madly to suck on them. Gently stroking Hal's hair, Jurgita positioned the mounds, so dazzling and fair, so voluptuous and lovely, at Hal's mouth.

"You look just like the 'cousin' I married," she murmured. "The night before he left in search of Užupis, I suckled him then as I suckle you now."

As hot tears streamed from her eyes, the tenor's song soared to a grand finale.

CHAPTER 10 Poets of a Colonized Land

Hal awoke to find Jurgita's head nestled in his bosom. She looked like a little bird shuddering in the cold. Hal wondered how long she had been awake. Maybe she hadn't slept, was waiting for him to awaken?

"I'll be back. I'm going to find our fatherland and then come back for you," said Hal.

"That's exactly what my husband said. He promised he'd take me to Užupis. But he never came back."

Hal sat up in bed. "I won't do that, Jurgita. I will live to see the day that I find our great country—absolutely!" So saying, Hal jumped out of bed and began to dress.

"But how?" asked Jurgita.

"There has to be a way. I'm thinking of asking Urbonas."

Jurgita lurched up, startled. Quickly she gathered her clothes and began to dress, grave worry evident on her face.

"What in heaven's name is wrong with that?" asked Hal.

"Nothing's wrong, it's just he's someone you can't possibly meet." Jurgita finished dressing and continued, "Do you really know who Urbonas is? Do you know how long ago he was in Siberia—where, it's said, he died?"

"But I saw him the night before last," said Hal. "On my way back to the hotel from Eigis's."

This brought a hysterical giggle from Jurgita. "So, you saw Urbonas. Urbonas, risen from the dead. My husband said the very same thing." She clapped a hand to her forehead in despair. After a long silence she murmured, "Poor Urbonas. How he must have longed for his fatherland, coming back to look for it even in death—and still he can't find it ..."

"What in heaven's name are you saying?" Hal barked.

"What am I saying?" Jurgita echoed. And then her tone hardened. "I'm saying Urbonas is dead. But if you want to see him, you don't have to go out in the cold. I wouldn't be surprised if he's still out there." Hurrying to the window, she flung open the curtains. "Come, look. There he is. Doesn't realize it's almost dawn."

Hal approached the window and looked out. Everything was cloaked in gloom. But there, at the corner of the alley, was a tall man, standing like a statue in the falling snow. Hal recognized him. As the first rays of dawn struck the man, he began to grow faint.

"So what do I do now?" Hal mumbled, still staring out the window.

"Can't you just stay here?" Jurgita ventured.

"No, I can't. I need to bury my father's ashes."

Jurgita heaved a sigh, and now it was she who mumbled. "Men always have to leave. My husband had to leave. It's the fate of the men of Užupis."

Hal donned his overcoat, gloves, and hat, hefted his suitcase, and opened the door.

When Hal had gone, Jurgita began to sob silently.

As Hal was crossing the snow-filled courtyard of the apartment building a cathedral bell began to toll. The sound lacked the brilliance of a new bell but was loud enough to make Hal's ears ring. The sudden tolling sent a flock of pigeons winging frantically into the sky.

Hal didn't realize how close the cathedral was until he emerged from the courtyard and rounded the corner. There it was. Hal looked up toward the steeples, trying to locate the source of the clamor. But all he saw against the gray backdrop of clouds was the crown-shaped cluster of steeples and above it myriad falling flakes of snow. The origin of the persistent tolling remained a mystery.

Just then Hal noticed an old woman squatting in front of the cathedral. She was munching on something, jaws hard at work. Spotting Hal, the woman shot to her feet and scudded over to him, and began a swooning chatter, all the while making the sign of the cross before him. Finally Hal recognized her—the beggar woman he had come across on his way to Eigis's party with André and the others.

"Grandmother!" Hal rejoiced. "We meet again! Aren't you cold?"

But the old woman understood not a word of Hal's English and continued to chatter on. Hal saw in her hand what she had been eating—kernels of corn, perhaps, or maybe they were sunflower seeds. Hal held out his hand to stem her steady stream of prattle.

"Grandmother, what *are* you eating? Could you give me some?"

The old woman's babble stopped and with a bashful smile she emptied the contents of her palm into Hal's. Hal inspected the small kernels—were they actually tiny, shriveled-up fruit?—then placed one of them in his mouth and chewed slowly and carefully. Whatever it was, it had a distinctive taste, unlike that of corn, sunflower seeds, or fruit. "It's good," he said. And then he sampled half a dozen more, savoring the kernels. And then a dozen more, and by now he was chomping away. The old woman looked on approvingly and began to yack once again, but Hal understood not a word of it. He popped the remaining kernels into his mouth. At the same time, he took out his wallet, assuming the woman would ask for a donation, like last time. But when she saw the wallet, the old woman's face hardened—no, she wasn't expecting payment. Her stern disposition made Hal hesitate, but only for a moment, after which he produced a ten-*litas* note.

"It's all right, grandmother, take it. I have more than enough for what I need." But the old woman flatly refused, and instead resumed her endless chatter. She was even more serious now.

Hal was at a loss. Just then he heard a voice.

"Hal! Here you are! What are you doing?"

Hal turned and there was dark-eyed Alvydas. "Alvydas! You're just in time—could you tell me what in heaven's name this lady is saying?"

Alvydas began talking with the old woman. She spoke with the same serious expression, Alvydas nodding in reply. Presently Alvydas turned back to Hal.

"She is saying she accepted a hundred *litas* from you the other night and she cannot accept any more. And in return for all that money you gave her, she would like to extend you a blessing."

"A blessing?"

"Yes—she wants to tell you your fortune. We have quite a

few of these old fortune tellers, but hardly any of them are ever accurate."

Hal shrugged in embarrassment.

The old woman said something more, and suddenly Alvydas broke out laughing.

"She says you are the grandfather of the holy maiden Jeanne d'Arc, that you will meet your granddaughter and she will be the savior of your homeland."

"What could she possibly be talking about?" said Hal.

Alvydas shrugged, just as perplexed as Hal.

The woman said something more.

"A good wife nurtures swallows," Alvydas interpreted. "And swallows nurture good citizens."

"And what's that supposed to mean?" asked Hal, even more confounded.

"I do not know any more than you," said Alvydas.

Concerned, the old woman reached up and once again made the sign of the cross above Hal's face. Again she spoke.

"What now?" said Hal, still feeling awkward.

Now it was Alvydas who looked uncomfortable. He led Hal off. "Never mind what she is saying. Let us go. How about a hot drink?"

Off the two men walked. But something was nagging at Hal. "What was she saying at the end, just now?"

"Do not worry." And then in a displeased tone: "When you flash your money around like you did the other night, the beggars will flock to you."

Embarrassed, Hal was momentarily silent. "Well, I'm sorry if I gave you that impression. It's just that when I saw that old woman the other night, she reminded me of my mother."

Alvydas kept a frosty silence.

Hal followed Alvydas into Café Mano and they settled themselves at the table where Hal and Rimas had sat. The awkward silence continued. And then Alvydas grabbed a program from his pocket along with a ticket. "Would you come see my play tonight? I wrote and produced it; it has been playing for a month now. But it closes tonight—so this is your last chance to see it."

"How wonderful," said Hal carefully, "but would I be able to understand the play?"

Alvydas nodded sympathetically. "Perhaps not—but somehow I think you might."

"What's the play about?"

"It is called *Poets of a Colonized Land;* I adapted it from a poem."

"*Poets of a Colonized Land?*" said Hal, alarmed. You mean Urbonas's poem?"

Alvydas shook his head firmly. "No, it is by the Ukrainian poet Yorslav."

"No, no," said Hal. "It was written *about* Yorslav. Urbonas was the Poet of the People of the Republic of Užupis during the colonial period, and his poem mourns the death of Yorslav, because Ukraine was in the same situation as Užupis. Yorslav was assassinated because of a plot he was involved in. The poem brought the people of Ukraine to tears and lit the fire that became their independence movement."

"Yorslav was *not* assassinated," replied Alvydas in exasperation, his tone gruff as never before. "He did not die until the year before last, after Ukraine became independent. He died in a car fire—he was driving on the expressway."

"Maybe you're right," said Hal, intimidated, "but I wonder if we're talking about two different poems with the same title."

"What in God's name is your poem by Urbonas about anyway?"

Discouraged by Alvydas's persistence and irritation, Hal could only murmur, "Well, as far as I know, it's about how all the poets in a colonized land are left-handed ... and all their daughters are mute ... and—"

"The next thing you're going to tell me," broke in Alvydas in a touchy tone, "is that Cervantes wrote *Hamlet*. You're saying Urbonas wrote that poem? No—*Yorslav* wrote it."

Hal gaped at Alvydas.

Suddenly Alvydas lost his temper. "What in hell have you been up to with Vilma, anyway?" he barked.

"What are you talking about?" said Hal in amazement. "I haven't done anything with her."

"Nothing? Then tell me, why do you suppose she cut her wrists last night?"

Hal blanched.

Alvydas kept up the attack: "Where were you last night? I went several times to the Hotel Užupis, but you weren't there."

Dazed, Hal finally replied, "What happened to Vilma?—tell me."

"Fortunately she is alive. Thank God they found her before it was too late ..."

Hal heaved a sigh of relief. "Where is she now?"

"In the hospital."

Hal lapsed into a pained silence. "Would it be all right if I saw her?" he ventured after a while.

"Absolutely not," said Alvydas. "That would be an insult to her."

"That's not my intention at all," said Hal desperately. "I just wanted to—"

But Alvydas cut him off.

"Of course—it's not your *intention*, you just want to *comfort* her. Just like you want the pleasure of knowing how superior you are when you shell out a hundred *litas* to every beggar in Vilnius. Did it ever occur to you, that to a woman whose pride has been injured on account of you, a visit by you might be considered yet one more insult?"

Mortified, Hal could say nothing.

Alvydas pressed on: "Well, am I wrong?"

"No," said Hal, waving his hands placatingly. "No, what you say makes sense, but—"

And, yet again, Alvydas interrupted.

"But what? You will marry Vilma like you promised her?"

"For the love of God will you hear me to the end? I never promised to marry Vilma. And I couldn't even if I wanted to, because—"

Again Alvydas interjected.

"Then why did you go to the Office for Foreign Nationals and take out a marriage certificate with her?"

Hal's head slumped forward—where to begin? Presently he looked up.

"If you'll just hear me out, you'll see you've misread the situation. The reason I went to the ministry was *not* to get a marriage certificate; I went to get a visa extension. Because I entered this country without a visa, I can only stay here forty-eight hours—that's what they told me. But when I got there I ran into Vilma—I never expected to see her there. And—"

One last interruption. "I know, I know. I read all about it." So saying, Alvydas produced a folded sheet of paper and an envelope, and offered them to Hal. To Hal's surprise, it was the correspondence he had left for Rimas at the hotel. Hal accepted the letter and envelope but was too upset to say anything.

"Yes, I realize it is wrong of me to read someone else's correspondence, but thanks to that letter, my misunderstanding with you is cleared up. And I am no longer resentful toward you. But having said that, I still want to know where the hell you were last night." Alvydas sounded like a detective grilling a suspect.

To Hal it was preposterous. "So the misunderstanding is cleared up—I guess I should be grateful. But I don't think that gives you the right to interrogate me as to my whereabouts last night."

Alvydas could no longer contain the anger seething inside him. "Would you like to know the last thing that old woman told me?" he screamed, barely coherent. "She said that tonight you would go to Užupis. You would cross to the far side of the river. What river do you suppose she meant? I'll bet my last *litas* that you would never guess the Vilnia." He paused for a moment and then his voice dropped to a murmur. "Maybe that is the one she meant. When Napoleon crossed that river he could not turn back—his doom was sealed." But the next moment he seemed at a loss, flustered by his own vehemence.

Hal observed him silently.

"I am sorry," said Alvydas. "I am not sure why I am so on edge. Maybe it is Vilma's suicide attempt. Whatever, I am not in my right mind. I am sorry." He brusquely rose. "The play is at the Municipal Theater, and the curtain goes up at eight. You will find a map inside the program. Do you think you will come?"

Hal replied that he would be sure to go if at all possible.

"All right, I will see you tonight, then." And he prepared to head out. But in front of the bar he bumped into a fortyish man in a suit. The man's attire was as flawless as a bridegroom's; in fact, he was perfect in every respect—his intelligent demeanor, his height, his good looks, his restrained smile. At the very least he must be a high-ranking Lithuanian government official destined for great things.

Alvydas shook hands with the man. If Alvydas was delighted to see the man, the man was ecstatic to see Alvydas, whom he gave a friendly pat on the back. They commenced a conversation, in which Alvydas gave every indication of being a longtime admirer of Mr. Handsome, who in turn seemed to regard Alvydas with profound trust. And on they talked, unpretentious and without affectation. At one point Mr. Handsome gestured toward the coffee urn, whereupon Alvydas checked his watch and shook his head, and they resumed their conversation, remaining at the entrance to the cafe. Engrossed in whatever it was they were talking about, they grew oblivious to their surroundings. But then Alvydas pointed several times to Hal, sitting by himself, whereupon Mr. Handsome himself cast several glances at Hal, laughing disdainfully. Alvydas laughed along with him.

Hal wondered if he had become the object of Alvydas's scorn, if Alvydas was telling Mr. Handsome about Hal's insistence that 'Poets of a Colonized Land' had been written by Urbonas. Disconcerted by the two men laughing and sneering at him, Hal gazed vacantly out the window. There was only the brick wall, looking denuded where the mortar had come out, and the falling snow, impervious to all. The scene was monotonous and claustrophobic, and when Hal turned back toward the door, the two men were still talking and glancing in his direction.

Just then cute Zoja appeared. Flashing a smile, she asked if Hal would like to order something. A *pálinka*, Hal replied. Zoja returned, still smiling, to the bar. While he waited for her Hal opened the program for the play. The text was in Lithuanian and the lettering was dense. Hal leafed through the pages looking for photographs. The first one was of Alvydas himself, dressed in black, face square and severe. Hal studied the photo, then looked up to compare that Alvydas with the one near the door. Alvydas was still talking with Mr. Handsome, and Mr. Handsome was still laughing.

Hal turned the page and saw a middle-aged man. He looked to be a man of substance, generous of spirit, and he had a refined smile. Hal wondered if he directed the Municipal Theater, or else was artistic director of the company that performed there.

The next page showed a younger man, perhaps in his early forties. He had a pale face and bushy hair. He was tight-lipped and he looked dead ahead, his eyes projecting the fierceness of a beast. This must be the lead actor. Hal's eyes lingered on this man, and then he turned the page.

Here was an actress who looked to be in her mid-thirties. She gazed vacantly toward the camera, chin cupped in her palm, her face ridden with exhaustion. This had to be Sophie, the French ballerina whom Hal had met at Eigis's.

While Hal was looking at Sophie, cute Zoja returned with his *pálinka,* beamed at him, and set down the drink.

"Zoja," said Hal, "after the last time, did you see my Belarus friend, Rimas?"

Zoja flashed her smile and shook her head, no.

Hal was disappointed. "Then could you please tell him something if he comes here? Could you tell him, 'Hal wants you to leave him a message at the hotel'?"

Zoja listened, blinking, then flashed her smile and nodded before turning back toward the bar. To get to the bar meant passing by the entrance, where Alvydas and Mr. Handsome were parked. Mr. Handsome intercepted her and asked a question. Cute Zoja shrugged. With a glance at Hal Mr. Handsome followed with a second question. Cute Zoja looked in Hal's direction reluctantly, then said something. Hal wondered if Mr. Handsome was prying into their conversation. Anxiously, Hal buried his face in the program.

The photo on the next page was a scene from the play. A fortyish man with a huge suitcase stood waiting for a bus beside a highway that stretched out through a desolate expanse. How could a stage set look so realistic, like a real-life backdrop in a film shoot? Hal looked up, thinking he would ask how Alvydas had managed that. But Alvydas had disappeared, and Mr. Handsome too. Hal looked about the café, but saw no trace of either man. Bottoms up! he told himself, and he drained his shot of *pálinka*.

Finally Hal could relax. Returning to the program, he saw on the next page a black-and-white photo of a young man with a stylish mustache. Was this the poet who had written 'Poets in a Colonized Land'—the basis for the play? The delicate corners of the man's mouth were drawn up into a smirk—he must have been a Don Juan. The image was streaked and of poor quality—it must have been an old photo.

Hal gazed at the photo for the longest time, then folded the program, put it in his pocket, and rose. Before leaving the café he checked one last time with Zoja, asking her to be sure to tell Rimas to leave him a message at the hotel. Zoja beamed and nodded.

CHAPTER 11 **Marija, the Flower Girl**

Leaving Café Mano, Hal struck out for the hotel. When he arrived the receptionist called out to him: "A man named Alvydas came looking for you last night—he must have been here three or four times."

Hal said he was aware of that. Had anyone else come looking for him?

No, said the young man.

Hal asked for an envelope and placed inside it his message and letter to Rimas. Writing "To Rimas" on the outside, he handed the envelope to the receptionist.

"Please make sure you give this only to Rimas—no one else."

"All right," said the young man before locking the envelope in a drawer.

Hal had just stepped back outside when a girl crouched at the entrance sprang to her feet in front of him. She looked jubilant; she must have been waiting for him. Aha, she was the girl from two nights ago, when he had returned to the hotel. He bent down so that he was at eye level with her.

"What are you doing here? There aren't many people buying flowers at this time of day ... You weren't dozing off, were you, hunched up in the cold like this?"

Instead of answering, the girl reached in her pocket, produced a handful of coins and bills, and held them out to Hal.

"What's this?" said Hal dubiously.

The girl launched into an explanation. But Hal understood not a word of it. Seeing his puzzled look, the girl started over, obviously frustrated, and this time marshaling all the languages at her command—Lithuanian, Russian, and Polish. But the result was the same: Hal didn't understand. In exasperation the girl blurted out something else:

"I'm trying to tell you that this is your change."

This time Hal understood, for the girl had spoken in Užupis. Hal squatted in front of her. "You speak Užupis?"

Even though Hal was speaking, as usual, in English, the girl nodded, then continued in Užupis: "My grandmother told me that two hundred *litas* is way too much for a flower. She told me I had to give you back some money."

Hal was so astonished, and so proud of the girl, that he could only ask, "Where in heaven's name did you learn Užupis?"

Instead of answering, the girl took Hal's hand and wrapped his fingers around the money. "There—it's yours." She looked relieved to have returned the money.

Clutching the girl's wrist, Hal said, "I told you the other night—this is my gift to you; I can't take it back." And he put the money back in the girl's hand.

The girl was at a loss. "I told you, my grandmother said I had to give it back to you." She was clearly a bright child, able to maintain a semblance of a conversation even though she didn't understand Hal's words.

"But you see," Hal practically pleaded, "I'm going to the Republic of Užupis, so I won't need this money any more. For the love of God take it!"

The girl was taken aback. "Did you say Republic of Užupis?"

Hal nodded. "Yes, the Republic of Užupis." And then, in a pleading tone, "But I don't know how to get there."

"My grandmother knows the Republic of Užupis," said the girl.

Astounded, Hal placed his hands on the girl's shoulders. "What did you say?"

"My grandmother knows the Republic of Užupis."

"But how?"

"She used to live there."

"Where does your grandmother live now? Can I see her?"

These words the girl didn't seem to understand, for she followed up on her last utterance: "She said she used to live there."

Hal spoke more slowly and deliberately: "Where does your grandmother live now?"

This time the girl seemed more sure of herself. "Adutiskis."

"Adutiskis?"

"Yes, Adutiskis."

Hal made as if he were walking away. "Can you take me there?"

The girl merely gazed at Hal.

Thinking she hadn't understood, Hal repeated the question, and finally the girl answered.

"No, I can't. It's far away. And I have to sell my flowers."

"I'll buy your flowers. Just take me to Adutiskis," Hal pleaded.

Again the girl seemed not to understand. "No, I can't. Adutiskis is too far away. And I have to sell these flowers."

"I'll buy your flowers," Hal repeated, gesturing slowly so the girl would understand he meant to buy all of them.

But the girl stuck out her chin and shook her head. "No, I can't. Only one flower to a customer."

Hal lapsed into despair.

"But I can give you my grandmother's address."

Hal's face lit up. "You can?" he shouted. "Yes, do that." He handed the girl his fountain pen and memo pad.

The girl took the memo pad in her right hand, the pen in her left, and began deliberately to write. Hal noticed that for someone who wrote left-handed, her penmanship was clean and neat.

When the girl had finished, she gazed for a moment at the fountain pen before returning it to Hal along with the memo pad. "There's a fountain pen just like this where my grandmother lives."

Instead of responding, Hal gazed at what the girl had written.

"Your grandmother's name is Jurgita?"

The girl nodded.

"And what is your name?"

"Marija."

"Marija. Your name is Marija."

The girl nodded.

Just then a man emerged from the hotel. Thinking a hotel employee could give him directions, Hal called out, "Excuse me—could you tell me where Adutiskis is?"

The man considered a moment, then said, "It's near the border. If you'll give me a moment, I'll find a map for you."

While the man went back inside, Hal kept a firm grip on Marija's wrist, worried that the girl might fly off.

Presently the man returned with a map and pointed out the location of Adutiskis. Hal saw it was near the border with Belarus.

"It's about a hundred kilometers from here," said the man.

Hal thanked him.

"You're welcome," said the man, who then handed Hal the map before walking away.

Hal checked the location of Adutiskis once more, then looked up for Marija. But in that short interval she had indeed disappeared. Hal noticed, on top of his suitcase, the money she had wanted to return to him.

"Marija!" Hal called as he looked about. But she was nowhere in sight.

Just then a taxi came to a stop in front of Hal. The driver's-side window came down, revealing a white-haired man.

"Taxi, sir?"

The man's face looked familiar. "Good timing," said Hal.

The driver got out and loaded Hal's suitcase into the trunk. "Where to, sir?"

"Adutiskis."

"Adutiskis?" said the man, as if he had never heard of it before.

"Yes, Adutiskis." Hal handed the driver the address Marija had written.

The driver took out a pair of spectacles.

Well, what do you know? The fortyish man was Jonas from the airport, who had taken Hal for a ride—and then some.

"Okay, let's go!" said the man once he had inspected the address. He climbed back in and Hal followed suit. But when Jonas turned on the ignition, nothing happened. After several more fruitless attempts he opened the door, planted his left foot on the icy surface of the street, and began pushing. Fortunately the engine caught after only a few meters, whereupon Jonas quickly pulled his foot back inside, and off they went. Hal followed Jonas's every move with an appreciative grin.

As the taxi made a U-turn in front of the Hotel Užupis, Hal looked out for Marija. But the car window revealed only the falling snow.

The taxi crossed the small bridge, passed the Russian Orthodox church where Hal had seen Jurgita the previous day, and crossed a longer bridge. They were now in the outlying area of the city, where the monotonous apartment complexes from the Soviet period stretched off into the distance. This and all other sights were indistinct in the falling snow.

Before long they had left the city behind and were traveling through snowy woods. The white drapery of branches overhead felt like a tunnel bored through the snow. Occasionally Hal noticed a smaller tree that had collapsed under the weight of the snowfall. All was still, not even a bird in sight.

And then they were out of the woods and passing a succession of fields that, in spite of their white covering, bore signs of having been farmed. Hal realized the fields must continue into the far distance, where all was obscured by the falling snow.

Small villages appeared from time to time, only the outlines of the buildings taking shape in the mist, so that the structures seemed to float on air. There were no obvious signs of life. No sooner did they pass a village than there came into view low, rolling hills receiving the ceaseless fall of snowflakes from the endless expanse of gray sky.

Woods, fields, villages, hills—on went the taxi through this perennial landscape. Lost in thought, feeling numb, Hal kept to himself. The driver was silent as well, concentrating on his driving. The only sounds came from the car—the whine of the engine, the chain-clad wheels bumping along the snowy road, the rattling of the timeworn chassis, the wind hissing though gaps and crevices.

After some two hours of tedious silence the driver pulled the taxi to the side of the road midway through an expanse of fields. It looked like a bus stop, but there were neither passengers nor habitations in sight.

Jonas broke the silence: "Could I see that address again?"

"What?"

"The address."

Hal produced his memo pad, opened it to the page containing Marija's compact, precise script, and handed it to the driver. Jonas put on his glasses just long enough to check the address, then returned the glasses to his pocket and the pad to Hal.

"We're here."

Hal took in the surroundings with a dubious expression—he saw only fields, nothing else.

"What do you mean? There's nothing here."

"True enough. But we're here all right." So saying, Jonas got out and opened the trunk to unload Hal's suitcase.

"Jonas!" Hal shouted as he got out. "You're playing around with me again."

Jonas's head jerked around and his face took on a sheepish expression as he realized who his passenger was.

Hal kept up the offensive: "You played me for a fool the last time too. You drove me around for an hour just to get from the airport to the hotel. You figured you'd try the same trick today, didn't you?"

Jonas's face was the picture of innocence. "I am sorry about that, but it was not intentional. I am a professor, and I only drive a taxi as a side job—I simply got lost. But not this time—we are here, I am sure of it." He pulled Hal's suitcase from the trunk and set it on the snowy ground.

"Jonas!" Hal cried out in aggravation. "How can you call yourself a professor? You want me to believe that Adutiskis is *here*, in the middle of these fields?"

"Now look," protested Jonas. "Adutiskis is five miles down that road. But this is as far as the taxi goes—there is too much snow on the road. What else can I do?" So saying, he pointed out a junction ahead of them, where a road branched off.

Hal saw an expanse of virgin white stretching out into the distance, and at the junction a tiny sign, "Adutiskis, 5 miles." So much snow was on the road that there was indeed no way the ancient taxi could have navigated it. The snowy road bore no sign of traffic, only the patterned imprints of bird feet. Hal considered. "Are you sure it goes to Adutiskis?"

Jonas pointed to the sign. "That is what it says" was his blunt response.

"Is there any other way to get there?"

"No."

"You want me to believe that there are actually people living down that road?"

"Why not?"

"So what am I supposed to do?"

Jonas shrugged. "You have two choices—go the rest of the way on foot, or go back to Vilnius."

Hal felt a surge of anger at Jonas's matter-of-fact tone, but managed to suppress it.

"Go on foot—in this snow?"

Jonas shrugged again, as if this were none of his concern. "The fare to here is three hundred thirty *litas*. But if you want to go back to Vilnius, I'll settle for six hundred."

Hal, deciding that any further display of anger would be fruitless, took out his wallet, produced four hundred-*litas* bills, and handed them to Jonas. "Jonas, that is *so* kind of you."

Ignoring Hal's sarcasm, Jonas counted out change and offered it to Hal.

"Don't bother," said Hal in irritation. "You've earned it with your kindness. In fact, you're so kind it makes me sick."

"Oh, thank you," said Jonas. "Thank you so much. You are truly my friend. If you would like, I can wait here while you take care of your business in Adutiskis, and then I will take you back to Vilnius. Of course I would have to charge you additional for waiting."

"No thank you," said Hal coldly.

Jonas responded with a series of bows. "You are truly a gentleman, truly a good man. Thank you." And then he bustled back inside his taxi, swung it about, and departed as if he couldn't wait to leave.

The surroundings became deathly silent. Suitcase in hand, Hal stood beside the snowy road amid the empty expanse of fields. Some five minutes passed before he set out for Adutiskis. The going was almost impossibly difficult, his feet sinking deep into the snow with every step. The snow was knee deep, and in places thigh deep, such that Hal could only plunge ahead one painfully slow step after another, the effort requiring all his energy. There was no place to rest, and the only signs of life on the snowy road were the bird tracks.

After an hour Hal caught sight of a hut-like structure and floundered toward it as best he could. Up close he saw it was a bus stop. Wind-driven snow had accumulated inside, but the three walls and the roof offered a modicum of shelter, and there was also a bench. Hal pushed aside enough snow to make room to sit.

Just then a man appeared from the same direction whence Hal had come; he was toting on his back a huge grandfather clock.

Hal jumped to his feet, ecstatic. "Hello, sir!" he called out. "Where are you going?"

But the man took no notice of Hal and marched past him in silence.

Hal scampered out onto the snowy road and intercepted the man. "Where are you going?" he shouted. "Are you going to Adutiskis?"

Instead of stopping, the man turned abruptly left and off the road, and made straight for a hill.

"Why don't you answer?" Hal shouted after him. "Are you hard of hearing? Can you speak?"

The man continued on as if Hal didn't exist, plodding through the snow-covered farmland toward the hill. Soon he was up to his waist, and as he floundered along, Hal became worried that a wrong step would send him plunging headlong into the snow.

"Come back!" he shouted. "I'm not going to bother you!"

But he heard only the echo of his voice. Without a backward look the man continued to plow ahead toward his destination. Presently he reached the foot of the hill and began to climb.

There was nothing for Hal to do but return to the bus stop. And there he sat, gazing at the surreal spectacle of the man with the heavy clock on his back going up the hill.

Presently the man arrived at the crest of the hill, where he set down his clock. Hal saw the man open the cover and concluded he was going to wind it. But instead, out flew a flock of birds, and with a clamor of chirping they formed a dark cloud in the sky. The man's gaze followed the flock upward. Greatly amused, Hal cackled madly. The echoes resounded all the more for the emptiness of the snow-covered landscape.

Finally Hal came back to his senses. Hefting his suitcase, he resumed his journey.

CHAPTER 12 The Swallows in the Drawers

Hal had lost track of how long he'd been walking, when he came across a small chapel beneath a burly, oriental oak. Inside, candles were burning—someone had been here not long before. Outside, a path had been cleared toward the fields. Did it lead to a town nearby?

As Hal was catching his breath he noticed a boy walking toward him along the path. He was carrying a rabbit, which he held thoughtfully against his cheek. *How dear*, thought Hal. He could just barely make out, behind the boy, the silhouette of a village.

"Young fellow!" Hal cried out in delight as he rushed toward the boy. "Is this Adutiskis?"

The boy's jaw dropped. And why not—Hal was a stranger popping out of nowhere, huge suitcase in hand, head and shoulders draped in snow.

"Don't be scared—it's all right!" Hal shouted, retreating a few tactful steps.

The boy gaped at Hal.

"I'm looking for Jurgita—Marija's grandmother, Jurgita."

The boy's face was frozen in fright. Communication was impossible. Hal grew desperate.

"For the love of God, say something! Do you know where Marija's grandmother lives? I have to find the Republic of Užupis. Do you know where it is?"

Hearing this, the boy shrieked, tossed the rabbit onto the snow-cushioned ground, and ran off toward the village. The rabbit eyed Hal warily, then hopped off over the snow.

"Dammit—stupid bumpkins," Hal grumbled despondently. And then he floundered off after the boy. Having already plowed through the snow and endured the cold for a good two hours, Hal felt giddy, and the village off in the distance became a mirage, floating on air.

A group of rustics had gathered just outside the village, anticipating the stranger's arrival—seniors, farmers, housewives, half a dozen boys, and, for a good measure, a few dogs. Curious and vigilant, they watched the intruder approach. They caught the mood of their masters and began yelping.

Cold and hungry, by the time Hal reached them he was ready to collapse.

"Hello. Is this Adutiskis?"

The question was greeted with a roar of laughter.

Hal grew apprehensive—it was like trying to communicate with ghosts.

And then a boy began to mimic him. "Hello!" he sang out. Again the villagers burst into laughter.

Hal wondered if his English sounded funny. He tried to smile, but his frozen face grimaced instead. Once again he asked if this was Adutiskis, and once again the villagers broke out laughing.

"Jurgita, Marija's grandmother—where can I find her?"

This time the villagers chattered among themselves. The boy who had mimicked Hal began repeating Jurgita's name to the grownups. And then another boy jabbed his finger toward the village and said something to Hal. Hal caught the name Jurgita and saw the boy pointing.

"Jurgita—over there?" asked Hal, pointing in the same direction.

"Okay!" called out a third boy, and again the villagers cracked up.

"Thank you!" said Hal.

The third boy copied him: "Thank you!"

By now the villagers were falling over themselves in laughter. And Hal finally realized the laughter came from merriment. The boys were exultant. Beckoning Hal, they led the way. Hal staggered along behind them and the adults brought up the rear, loath to miss out on the rare spectacle.

The village stretched out on both sides of the road. The dwellings were pretty much the same—squat, one-story wooden structures. Most were painted a drab, dark color; a few were the color of sienna. All were bordered by low fences, and behind them were fuzzy white outlines that could have been flower gardens or vegetable plots.

By now Hal's train had expanded to a few dozen as he followed the boys along the snowy road through the village. The newer arrivals included a farmer clutching a large goose, an elderly man tottering along beneath a black umbrella, and hobbling industriously with the aid of a crutch, was a frail young man. The boisterous parade brought others to the windows of their homes, where they parted thick curtains and stared bug-eyed through the glass.

Finally the boys came to a stop before one of the houses and they all began to talk at once, competing for Hal's attention.

"This is it?" Hal asked.

"Okay," said one of the boys. More laughter, and then all began calling for Jurgita—or so Hal concluded, for this name was the only word he understood. At the first pause, one of the boys called out, "Hello! Jurgita! Hello! Hello!" This time there was a chorus of chuckles.

In spite of the clamor, no one came to the door. In unison the villagers began chanting Jurgita's name, while some of the boys went around to the side of the house and tapped on a window. Finally the door opened and out poked the head of an old woman. She had blond hair and a radiant smile. It was amazing—the old woman looked just like young Jurgita from last night in Vilnius, only fifty years older.

The appearance of the old woman brought the assembly to a breathless silence.

Hal walked up to her. "How do you do? Are you Jurgita, grandmother of Marija?"

The woman fixed her scintillating smile on Hal. She seemed not to have understood Hal's English. The villagers guffawed. They must have anticipated difficulties in communication.

"I want to ask you about the Republic of Užupis." Hal articulated the words as slowly as possible.

"Užupis?" The old woman was alarmed.

"Yes, the Republic of Užupis."

"Then, you must understand the Užupis language?"

To Hal's surprise, he was indeed able to understand; the old woman was speaking Užupis.

Hal nodded, ecstatic.

"Then let's go inside," said the woman with her effulgent smile. "It's cold out."

"Thank you."

After stamping his feet on the mat outside the door, Hal went in. The villagers looked on dubiously, confounded in their assumption of a language barrier between the odd foreigner and Jurgita.

Inside, Hal heard fluttering overhead. Were there birds in the house? It was impossible to tell, the interior was so dim. And Hal's eyes hadn't adjusted from his hours out in the blinding white snow.

"How did you ever get here, with the road snowed in? Don't tell me you walked in from the highway," said Jurgita.

Hal nodded as he removed hat, muffler, and coat, luxuriating in the warmth.

"For heaven's sake—all this way! Please, come and sit."

Hal sat down at an impressive table. The woman disappeared into the gloom to hang up Hal's garments. Coughing, Hal looked about. But it was too dark to see the layout or the furnishings, except for a clay *pechika* fireplace the color of sienna. A fire had been lit, and the interior was toasty. Hal scratched at his hands, feet, ears, and nose. The sudden warmth had brought life back to his numb extremities, inducing in them first a tingling and then a furious itching. His hacking cough continued.

The woman reappeared. "For goodness' sake! If we'd left you out any longer, you'd have frostbite by now," she said when she saw Hal scratching madly at himself. And then she went outside, calling "Kornelius! Kornelius!" A lanky boy emerged from the assemblage of villagers and trotted up to Jurgita, who sent him dashing off on an errand. As she returned inside, Hal again heard the flapping of wings.

"The first thing we need to do is thaw you out so you won't be frostbitten," said the woman as she brought Hal a large basin of cold water. To the basin she added hot water until she had achieved the desired temperature, and then she sprinkled in something—was it salt?—and stirred. She periodically tested the temperature while waiting for Kornelius, and by and by the boy returned. In his hand was a bottle containing a reddish liquid.

"Thanks, Kornelius," said the old woman as she accepted the bottle.

"You're welcome," said the boy. "Is there anything else you'd like me to do, Jurgita?"

Hal was surprised: the boy was speaking Užupis.

"No, I guess not. Run along now, and make sure the door's shut tight."

Reluctantly the boy left, and once again Hal heard the flapping of wings.

"That boy speaks Užupis too!" said Hal. But Jurgita was intent on mixing the contents of the bottle into the water. Before long a pungent rose fragrance issued from the potion. Was it rose extract that Kornelius had brought?

"That boy's mother, Laura, is originally from Belarus, just across the border. She got pregnant out of wedlock, and was afraid of what her father and brother would do, so she ran away and came here to have the baby. She claimed *Urbonas* was the father. Urbonas, dead and buried all these years—how could it be? Anyway, she asked me to take care of the boy, and that's how he learned Užupis." Jurgita paused to test the temperature of the water. "All right, it's ready now. Put your hands and feet in. It's an Užupis folk remedy. All it takes is five minutes, and then you won't have to worry about frostbite."

Hal removed his socks and shoes, coughing as he did, and stuck his feet in the basin. The water was lukewarm. And then he put his hands in. Sure enough, the prickly sensation in his extremities gradually eased. Hal bent over the bowl and splashed water on his itchy ears and nose as well.

Jurgita, meanwhile, spread a tablecloth and set the table with a soup bowl and spoon. Then she disappeared into the gloom, reappearing shortly after with a huge urn of soup.

"Why don't you dry yourself and have a nice hot bowl of

soup." So saying, the woman brought Hal a large towel.

Hal dried his hands and feet, then drew close to the table.

"Hot soup is just what you need for your cough," said the woman as she ladled the steaming liquid into the bowl.

"Thank you." Hal was exhausted and he tucked into his soup with the alacrity of a starving man. Jurgita stood beside him, looking on approvingly as he slurped the soup, unmindful of all else. Hal looked up at her. "Absolutely delicious. But whatever is in it? It has a jasmine fragrance."

The woman seemed not to have understood Hal's English. "Soup is just the thing for a cough. There's more, so help yourself." And with that she ladled more soup into Hal's bowl.

Hal had more soup and presently his coughing stopped.

"It's strange," Hal said. "I think I've had this soup before—it was delicious then too—but I can't remember when or where."

The woman seemed to understand none of this. Taking a huge loaf of bread from the basket on the table, she began slicing it into manageable hunks. Hal took a piece, dipped it in the soup, and ate. The woman looked on in satisfaction.

Suddenly Hal heard chortling. He looked toward the door. It was open a crack—the children must have been peeking in.

"Darius," scolded the woman. "Close that door—you're letting the cold in."

The next instant the door had clunked shut. And with the shutting of the door, Hal once more heard the flapping of wings.

"Those boys are a handful," said the woman. "They don't really have anywhere to go in winter, and they get stir crazy."

Maybe not just the boys, thought Hal, as he imagined them giving a detailed report on the Asian stranger having soup at Grandmother Jurgita's. And he imagined those among the grownups who had tasted Jurgita's delicious soup smacking their lips in appreciation. And he imagined other adults questioning the boys with staid and earnest looks. Children and grownups alike must have been bored to death with the winter itch.

When Hal had finished his soup, Jurgita brought him a hot cup of tea. "So you're a man of the Republic of Užupis," she said.

Hal nodded. "Yes. And I came to visit. But I don't know where Užupis is. That's why I've come to see you." Jurgita was not understanding, but Hal continued nevertheless. "I heard from Marija that you used to live in Užupis. Could you tell me where it is?"

But the woman could not grasp Hal's words. Flashing her resplendent smile, she said, "I used to speak English back in the old days. But after my husband left for Užupis, I stopped. That was fifty years ago, and now I don't understand the language—I've forgotten it all."

"Whatever became of your husband?" Hal pressed her.

The woman smiled her brilliant smile.

Just then Hal heard, from the dark recesses of the living room, the flapping of wings. He saw a pair of birds dart past him and he flinched.

"What are those?"

With a sheepish grin the woman pointed toward the mantle of the *pechika*. Hal saw there a cluster of nests, each with a huddle of chicks gazing at him intently.

"They're swallows!" he gasped, gazing back at the birds.

"When my Gerdihal died," said the woman, "I moved here from Vilnius. And the swallows came and built their nests."

"Swallows in the middle of the winter?" said Hal. "I can't believe it."

Jurgita led Hal by the hand to a child's desk at the side of the living room. The drawers were open; in each drawer was a nest, and in each nest were swallows. Some of the chicks gazed at Jurgita and cheeped softly.

"Good heavens!" said Hal.

"This is where they started," said old Jurgita. "It was Gerdihal's desk when he was a boy. When I first saw those nests I felt my boy had returned. But every year there are more little ones and now there are nests all over the house." So saying, she led Hal to the far wall, where a huge grandfather clock stood. The clock had stopped seemingly ages ago and the cover had fallen off, revealing more nests inside. Their occupants looked out sleepy-eyed at Hal.

"Simply amazing," he said.

"And there are more," said the old woman. "Come look." And she pointed out to Hal an old, broken violin resting on a shelf. Inside the violin were a pair of swallows looking out at them with somnolent eyes and twittering softly.

"This is the newest nest," said the woman. "Gerdihal used to play that violin. And now they've taken up residence."

"Just marvelous," said Hal.

"When spring comes, they're outside gadding about all day, and in winter they just keep to their nests. The little ones are absolute rascals, just like Gerdihal when he was a boy. So whenever I have a guest I keep it dark—that way they think it's nighttime and they stay nice and quiet in their nests."

Did that mean the thick curtains over the windows and the oppressive warmth in the living room were also for the benefit of the swallows?

"When they first started nesting here, I thought they would be gone come autumn. But they stayed. I guess it's so warm in here that they lost their seasonal instincts. So in winter I keep the fire going and that makes it nice and toasty for them."

Sure enough, there was a stack of firewood beside the *pechika*.

"The first few years I had Zamaitias to help me. He always made sure I had plenty of firewood before autumn arrived."

"Zamaitias? You mean the legendary hero of Užupis?" Hal asked incredulously.

But the woman didn't understand. "Young Kornelius has been helping me ever since Zamaitias died. But this coming spring, Kornelius is leaving. He wants to be a basketball player, so he's going to Vilnius. But what will happen to my poor babies after I die? That's what worries me."

She sounded forlorn, and Hal thought he would try to brighten her spirits. He had noticed a light switch on the wall. "I'm wondering exactly how many swallows you have here. Is it all right if I turn on the light?"

The woman nodded blissfully. Hal flicked the switch on. The living room brightened, and instantly the birds burst out in a clamor of chirping and took flight. From the mantle of the *pechika*, from the drawers, from the grandfather clock, from inside the violin, and from beneath the table they came, swarming dizzily about the living room.

"Good Heavens!" cried Hal. "This is really something!"

The woman looked proudly at the vigorous working of the birds' wings, her eyes gleaming, a smile filling her face. And then some of the swallows settled on her head and shoulders.

"Yes, yes," she said to the birds. "You can tell it's feeding time, can't you?" And then she poured feed into a trough beside the fireplace. The swallows flocked toward the trough, converging on it in a black mass. She then added water to their bowl.

In the light of the living room Hal could see that the swallows had taken over the house. Every nook and cranny held a nest, and beneath the nests the wooden floor was caked with milky excrement. Instead of a human habitation, the interior was a giant birdhouse—it was a mess.

Hal noticed a glass frame on the wall. "Oh, my!" he cried out. He approached the frame, entranced. "Isn't that the Užupis flag?" It was the very same flag he had seen in the apartment of young Jurgita in Vilnius last night. He gazed at it with tear-filled eyes as if he hadn't seen it in ages.

Old Jurgita had bent over to whisper to the birds. Was she reminding them to behave now that they had a visitor?

CHAPTER 13 Jurgita of Adutiskis

"It was left to me when my husband died," said Jurgita as Hal looked up at the flag.

"You've kept it all these years," Hal marveled.

"You are an Užupis man for sure if you recognize the flag," said Jurgita. "You're the very first man of Užupis I've met since Zamaitias died." After a forlorn pause, she said, "I have something to show you. Please follow me." Taking Hal's hand, she led him down a dark hall. All along, Hal heard the fluttering of wings. At the end of the hall Jurgita opened a door.

Behind it was a spacious room, clean and orderly. Hal saw several display cabinets containing photographs and a variety of objects. Light from outside came in through the uncurtained window, and there was a sheen to the wood floor. But unlike in the living room, there was a nose-tingling chill to the air.

"It's like a little museum!" said Hal. He looked about—where to begin? His eye was drawn first to one of the far cabinets, which contained a large flag identical to the one in the living room. Hal gazed at it, enchanted.

"Zamaitias gave me that flag just before he died," said Jurgita over his shoulder. Then she opened the cabinet and took out a small box that lay beneath the flag. Inside it was an old postcard. "Have a look—you can see the flag here too."

The black-and-white postcard showed a lake surrounding an ancient castle, from the steeple of which flew the flag of the Republic of Užupis. The grand castle was built of marble, and it rose against the backdrop of a snow-covered alpine range. Hal failed to notice it was the same postcard he had seen last night at the apartment of Jurgita in Vilnius.

"What a beautiful castle," said Hal.

"It's the presidential palace. A long, long time ago—I couldn't have been more than five—on that lawn you see there, I gave a bouquet to Zamaitias. Everyone had turned out to welcome him home after he won the Olympic marathon." Old Jurgita was steeped in sentiment as she went back in time.

"You actually met the legendary hero?" said Hal. He too was overcome with emotion.

Hal couldn't tell if she had understood his English, for she continued her story, displaying her shining smile. "The grownups pushed me toward him and I gave him the bouquet. He was wearing a laurel wreath and the flag was draped over his shoulders. He took that flag and wrapped it around *my* shoulders. I was too young to know better, and didn't realize the significance of it, and before long I'd forgotten all about it."

"So you actually met Zamaitias," Hal marveled.

"He was my father's adjutant," said Jurgita. "Always at my father's side. They went to war together. But after my father died in the war and we lost our country, Zamaitias turned to farming. He looked after me until the day he died—he always referred to me as 'Miss.' Before he breathed his last, he gave me that flag—the flag I had all but forgotten. He was such a good man—honest to a fault..."

She paused and made the sign of the cross. Hal noticed that she did so with her left hand.

"Who sent this postcard to whom?" Hal asked as he inspected the faint writing on the reverse.

This question old Jurgita seemed to have understood. "It was from Urbonas, the Užupis Poet of the People—he sent it to his nephew. At the time the nephew was in exile in a far-off land, and Urbonas wrote him this postcard telling him that our fatherland was once again independent and that he should come home."

Old Jurgita seemed to be recovering some of her long-forgotten English.

"Written in Urbonas's own hand—unbelievable," said Hal as he gazed at the postcard.

"And the nephew—he was my husband." Jurgita smiled blissfully. "And yet Laura, only thirty-two years old, claims that Urbonas is Kornelius's father—it's ridiculous. And it's not just Laura; every girl who gets pregnant out of wedlock says Urbonas is the father."

Hal chuckled. "I guess there's some truth to all these things I've been hearing about him!"

"I can understand those naïve girls," said Jurgita. "Any girl who read Urbonas's 'Mourning for Julia' must have dreamed she was in his arms making love with him. So I have no problem with them. What I *can't* tolerate are the people who claim they wrote his poems. As if Urbonas never existed!—it's outlandish. Some Russian scoundrel even had the nerve to translate Urbonas's poems into Russian and publish them under his own name."

"I met someone like that too!" Hal exclaimed. "He insisted that 'Poets of a Colonized Land' was written by a Ukrainian poet."

Jurgita sighed. "Urbonas once said that to regain our country is to regain our lost poetry."

These words gladdened Hal's heart. "My father said something similar," he murmured. "My honorable father—he said that to bury his remains in the Užupis homeland would be to plant the seeds of poetry." His eyes filled with tears.

To comfort him Jurgita retrieved a well-worn volume from a cabinet. "Shall I read you one of Urbonas's funniest poems?" So saying, she flipped through the pages with her left hand until she found the poem:

The gimpy postman sleeps inside his mail bag.
The blind doctor sleeps inside his medical satchel.
The dumb gypsy sleeps inside his violin case.
All people take with them a bag
In which to go to sleep.

In some kingdoms,
Japan, for example,
The people still go to sleep
Inside the shoes they wear.
But after the revolution
This is forbidden
In our village
And so the people have a bag at the ready instead.

Teary eyes and all, Hal began to giggle.

Old Jurgita chuckled as well, then continued:

Lacking a bag, I decided thus:
In the drawers of the swallows will I sleep.
Just as all of you have decided to sleep
With the frogs in the pot-bellied soup pot.
And just as your daughters have decided to sleep
With the matches in a matchbox.

Hal erupted in a belly laugh. His nose began to run. "That Urbonas sure is funny," he said, sniffling. "I wonder—did you ever meet him?"

Jurgita shrugged. "Not in person." And then, "Well, I might have." And finally, "Actually I did—yes, I'm sure of it." As evidence she indicated a photograph in one of the cabinets. "This is a photo of my husband's family, and Urbonas is in it."

In the center of the old black-and-white photo was a middle-aged man in full dress uniform, sitting stiff and stern, a medal pinned to his chest. Next to him sat a woman whose clothing bespoke refinement. Standing in front of the man and woman were a little girl and a tall boy who looked a couple of years her senior. And behind the middle-aged man and the woman was a thirtyish man, tall and with a stylish mustache, striking a pose for the camera. Judging from their dress and the elegant background, they must have been a dignitary and his family at the turn of the twentieth century. This photo was identical to the one Hal had seen last night at the apartment of Jurgita in Vilnius. But so intent was he on examining the individuals in the photo that this too escaped him.

"This was my father-in-law," said Jurgita, indicating the middle-aged man. "He was the Užupis ambassador to a faraway land, and after we lost our country he couldn't abide his sorrow and he took his own life."

"Good heavens," Hal lamented.

Jurgita remained composed. "He and my father were dear friends. So much so that I've always thought of those children of his as my cousins. And that 'cousin' there, he was a little older, he was my husband."

Hal nodded.

Indicating the tall, thirtyish man with the stylish mustache, old Jurgita continued: "And this is the famous Urbonas. At the time, I was playmates with my two 'cousins'—that boy and that girl." She then indicated the woman in the photo. "And I often went to her home for piano lessons. Which means I must have met Urbonas at some point. But it's been so long, I have no memory of it."

"That can happen," said Hal, nodding. "Memories are like fields at dusk: the ones in the distance are the first to disappear."

And now Jurgita nodded. Her long-forgotten English was continuing to awaken. "Oh, and here's my son Gerdihal," she said, pointing to a framed photograph in the next cabinet. The photo was of a young man, taken from the waist up. Looking straight at the camera, mouth clamped shut, he looked to be a man of conviction. His features were somehow Asian.

"After my husband left, Gerdihal was my only hope. He was so intelligent. He knew, not just Užupis, but Lithuanian, Russian, Polish, English, German, French—he spoke them all, free and easy. His writings were published in the newspapers of several countries." Retrieving a scrapbook from below the photograph, she spread it open before Hal.

"What a remarkable young man!" Hal exclaimed.

"And he made a point of translating Urbonas's poetry," Jurgita continued, "and his translations were published in several languages." She indicated a stack of books inside the cabinet.

"All of those books are your son's translations?"

Instead of acknowledging Hal's surprise, Jurgita murmured, "And then he died—he was only thirty-three."

"Oh no!" said Hal.

"He was killed in St. Petersburg."

"Good heavens!"

"Supposedly because he failed to assassinate the Russian czar."

"Oh no," Hal murmured, his tone filled with pain.

But Jurgita seemed to have gotten over her sorrow long ago.

Her glittering smile had returned. She regarded Hal and asked, "Are you understanding what I'm saying?"

Hal nodded vigorously. "Of course. I can't speak Užupis, but I have no problem understanding it."

But Jurgita remained dubious. "And here is my granddaughter, Marija," she said, indicating yet another photograph in the cabinet. In the photo, smiling from cheek to cheek, was the flower girl Hal had encountered.

"Ah, Marija. I met her this morning in Vilnius. She is one smart, cute girl."

"She's the daughter of Gerdihal and Julia."

Another incongruous answer, thought Hal.

Jurgita took the photo from the cabinet and caressed the image of the girl's face. Then she looked up at Hal. "After Gerdihal died, Julia ran off with the girl, all the way to Cordova."

"Cordova, in the south of Spain?"

Jurgita nodded. "Yes, all that distance. But she got homesick—the people of Užupis, it's in their blood. She threw herself off a bridge there and drowned."

"Oh no," Hal lamented. How could Jurgita remain so cruelly composed, gazing off into space.

"Threw herself off a bridge in Cordova," Hal mumbled. "It reminds me of a poem." He began to recite the poem, groping for the words:

Sometime, somewhere,
When we meet again,
We'll have an umbrella, waiting for the rain,
Rain like silver moonlight,
Rain like a blue sonata.

But in truth, we in this country
Have no season of rain.
And so the olive trees wither
The birds have ceased to sing
And your lips are parched.

Jurgita's translucent eyes were fixed on Hal, and he knew she understood this English-language poem.

Hal continued:

Sometime, somewhere, in a place like Cordova,
If we should meet again at the bridge in Cordova,
We'll pause as we cross it
To watch the wings of the butterflies
The fluttering wings of the yellow butterflies massing beneath the bridge
We'll watch the wings of the butterflies.

But in truth, we in this country
Have no sunny afternoons in spring
And so the fish remain still beneath the sheets of ice
And the buds of the flowers don't blossom
And your hands are always cold.

"Poor Julia—I wonder if she thought of that poem when she was on the bridge. Can you guess who wrote it?" Limpid tears had gathered in old Jurgita's eyes.

The question was unexpected, and Hal shrugged.

"Urbonas did. It was translated into English."

"Really! So 'Death on a Bridge in Cordova' was written by Urbonas! It's one of my favorite poems."

"And so Marija became an orphan. She arrived barefoot on my doorstep. I'll never forget how she looked that day—little Marija, barefoot at my door." Tears streamed down Jurgita's cheeks, but they could not extinguish her radiant smile.

Hal felt a swish of cold air.

"Darius!" Jurgita shrilled toward the window.

Hal saw boys' faces and noticed the window was open a crack. The next moment the faces were gone. Jurgita went to the window and closed it.

"The people here are kept captive by winter—nowhere to

go and nothing to entertain them. So to them you're like a circus clown."

Hal looked over Jurgita's shoulders and through the window. All he saw was the desolate expanse, no letup to the falling snow.

By now the boys peeping in would be done reporting to those grownups still gathered outside. About Jurgita showing the strange man the photos in her cabinets, explaining each and every one; about the man listening and nodding, and occasionally saying something in reply; about the man reciting a song—or maybe it was a poem—and about Grandmother Jurgita being brought to tears. Among the grownups would be those who listened in amazement and asked questions of the boys, and perhaps those who couldn't believe Jurgita and the stranger had actually been able to communicate, but also those infected by Jurgita's sorrow, their eyes grown bloodshot.

"I used to live in the city," said Jurgita to Hal. "But after Gerdihal died I came here. This is my father's ancestral home, and it's where Zamaitias lived as a farmer." A wave of emotion washed over her face as she contemplated these vicissitudes of time. Straining to sound playful, she pointed out another photograph and called out, "Ah, here we are—my husband!"

The photo showed Jurgita in her wedding dress, smiling in jubilation, together with her husband. Hal failed to notice that this photo, too, was identical to the one he had seen in the apartment of Jurgita in Vilnius.

"You're beautiful," gushed Hal, "and your husband is handsome and noble."

But old Jurgita seemed not to have understood. "He was my 'cousin,' a bit older than I, and he went into exile with his father. We were married after he returned. Until I die I'll never forget the day he came back."

Hal listened attentively.

"It was at the airport in Vilnius," she continued. "That same day, I had just come back from Denmark, and Zamaitias came out to meet me. He was a farmer then and he was holding a great big goose and he was wobbling the way a goose walks as he ran toward me on the icy street shouting 'Jurgita!' And who should hear him but my cousin, the cousin I had longed for day and night. He was on his way back to our newly liberated Republic of Užupis."

"Oh, how romantic," sighed Hal.

"But my 'cousin' didn't seem to recognize me. He had left when I was only six, and twenty years had passed. Can you blame him for not recognizing that six-year-old girl?"

Hal nodded.

"And can you believe it, the very next day I ran into him in the Orthodox church in Vilnius. The young women of today, they would have run into my cousin's arms—they wouldn't have tried to hide their joy. But me, how bashful I was then ... All I could do was ask him to meet me later at Café Mano. And then I sent Zamaitias there to fetch him home to me. I'm sure he had no clue I was his little cousin from years ago."

"Whatever became of your husband?" Hal felt compelled to ask.

Old Jurgita nodded as if she had understood Hal's question, albeit imperfectly. "The very next morning after he impregnated me with Gerdihal he left for Užupis. And he never did come back."

Hal looked heartbroken. He framed his next question carefully: "Did you perhaps resent him for that?"

A glowing smile lit up Old Jurgita's face. "You know we have this proverb in Užupis: 'If a man leaves home but doesn't achieve his goal, he must not come back alive.' And so I am proud of my husband. As was Gerdihal."

Hal nodded over and over.

Other memorabilia were carefully arranged in the cabinets: tuxedo, dress shoes, eyeglasses, fountain pen, medals. According to Jurgita, all had belonged to her father-in-law.

There was a knock on the window and a voice called out for Jurgita. She and Hal turned away from the display and saw, framed in the window, a large black umbrella that prevented them from seeing its owner. Snow was falling onto the umbrella. Jurgita went to the window, Hal following, and there beneath the umbrella was a short, elderly man looking up at them. Had the man heard that Jurgita was crying and wanted to comfort her?

"Mindaugas—you old fool!" said Jurgita as she opened the window. She switched to Lithuanian and squealed in protest at the old man, who responded with a servile grin and an attempt at an explanation. After a brief exchange, Jurgita closed the window. "Would you please excuse me a moment?" she said to Hal. "I need to show my face and tell these people what's happening, otherwise they'll be climbing the walls."

Jurgita left the room, and the clamorous chirping of the swallows came through the open door. Hal returned to the cabinets. He heard the front door open, followed by a round of applause. The assembly of villagers would be surrounding Jurgita, delighted that one of the objects of their curiosity had appeared. They would be competing to ask questions and then bobbing their heads. Hal imagined a question-and-answer session about the strange man: who was he, why had he come here, which language were they conversing in?

Hal resumed his inspection of the cabinets. There were: an old phonograph and some records; photos taken at a summer resort; a photo of a young Jurgita breast-feeding a baby, who must have been Gerdihal. And then Hal came across something unusual—a program for a play. Without thinking, he began to leaf through it.

The dense lettering was neither Russian nor English—it must have been Lithuanian. Hal turned the pages looking for photographs. There, a young man dressed in black was staring straight at the viewer, his face square and severe. On the next page, a middle-aged man. He looked to be a man of substance, generous of spirit, and he had a refined smile. Hal wondered if he directed the Municipal Theater, or else was artistic director of the company that performed there. The next page showed a younger man, perhaps in his early forties. He had a pale face and bushy hair. He was tight-lipped and he looked straight ahead, his eyes projecting the fierceness of a beast. This must be the lead actor. Hal's eyes lingered on this man, and then he turned the page. Here was an actress who looked to be in her mid-thirties. She gazed vacantly toward the camera, chin cupped in her palm, her face ridden with exhaustion. The photo on the next page was a scene from the play. A fortyish man with a huge suitcase stood waiting for a bus beside a highway that stretched out through a desolate expanse. How could a stage set look so realistic, like the real-life backdrop in a film shoot? The last page contained a black-and-white photo of a young man with a stylish mustache. Was this the playwright? The delicate corners of the man's mouth were drawn up in a smirk—he must have been a Don Juan. The image was streaked and of poor quality—it must have been an old photo.

Hal failed to notice the program was identical to the one Alvydas had given him that morning. As he was putting it back, an envelope bearing the words "To Rimas" caught his eye. Hal gazed at the envelope.

Just then Jurgita returned. Seeing the object of Hal's attention, she said, "Those are some letters my husband wrote to his friend Rimas."

Would it be all right if he had a look at them? asked Hal.

Jurgita took out the envelope and handed it to Hal.

Hal gingerly extracted the contents—three letters written in English. One was very short, the other two quite long. Hal started with the short one:

My good friend Rimas,

If by chance you stay in Vilnius another day, I would be grateful if you could leave me your local address. I will check back here from time to time to see if you have left me a message.

10:02 a.m.
Your friend

P.S. Vilma is indeed a woman of heavenly beauty.

Feeling like a peeping tom, he skipped the two long letters and returned all three to the envelope.

"If this man Rimas was going to Kishinev, then perhaps he's Moldovan?"

"Perhaps," said Jurgita. "But, come to think of it, I believe I heard someone say he's Estonian, a writer, and his brother was living in Moldova and fell ill and died, and, for the sake of his little nephew, Rimas married his brother's widow and I think they're living in Moldova."

"That reminds me," said Hal. "It was a custom in Užupis for a man to marry his brother's widow and help take care of the children."

Jurgita nodded. "Užupis people were very giving of themselves."

There remained one cabinet to inspect. Inside it Hal discovered a funeral portrait and beside it, wrapped in a black cloth, a container. In front of the funeral photograph were a medal and a revolver, and on top of the container rested a single red rose.

"And what are these?" Hal asked.

Jurgita explained: "Inside that urn are my father-in-law's ashes. He wanted them scattered in Užupis, so my husband brought them back from exile. But he died before he got to Užupis, and then Gerdihal died, and so the ashes never did make it back home. I'm waiting for the day Marija has a son who can spread those ashes."

Hal closed his eyes, trying to control his surging emotions. Tears began to seep out. To conceal them, he went to the window. Outside he saw only the snow falling onto the dreary expanse.

"Would you care to listen to some music?" said Jurgita to Hal's back.

But for Hal the words just wouldn't come.

Old Jurgita found a record and placed it on the turntable of the ancient phonograph. As Hal was wondering how the machine could possibly work, the turntable lurched into motion. With the hiss of static came music—a solemn and sorrowful prelude.

Hal's head jerked up. The prelude came to an end, and a tenor voice that managed to be both resonant and articulate began to sing the Užupis national anthem. Hal closed his eyes and grew rigid, overcome with fervor.

Oblivious to it all, the snow continued to fall on the desolate expanse outside.

CHAPTER 14 Down by the Vilnia River

Suitcase in hand, Hal emerged from Jurgita's house to find several boys kicking around something that looked like a Hacky Sack. The grownups must have gone inside to escape the cold.

When the boys saw Hal, they each began hollering "Hello!" Hal responded with a "Hello!" of his own. In utter delight the boys continued with an endless chorus of "Thank you!" and "Okay!" Hal gave a "Thank you!" in return. A couple of the boys scampered off to alert the grownups about Hal's departure.

Jurgita joined Hal. "Where will you go now?"

"To Užupis. Once I'm there, I'll notify you so you can re-visit the presidential palace, where you presented that bouquet to Zamaitias."

Jurgita radiated her brilliant smile and set off with Hal toward the outskirts of the village, retracing the route by which he had arrived. More villagers thronged the street. Not only the farmer with the huge goose, old Mindaugas with his black umbrella, and the young man clutching his crutch, but also a few musically inclined souls equipped with accordion or violin. Upon Hal's arrival they had followed him with mischievous curiosity, but now that he was leaving Hal sensed in them an endearing regret—especially when two of the musicians began a wistful song of farewell. The train of villagers grew solemn. Only the dogs were in a world of their own, romping about the snowy fields, tails wagging.

At the edge of the village Hal and Jurgita said their goodbyes. Each villager then bade Hal farewell in turn—the farmer holding the goose to his bosom, the elderly Mindaugas with his umbrella, and the young man clutching his crutch. Then each of the children shook hands with Hal. At the conclusion of their song, the two musicians did likewise. And then a farmer stepped forward and presented Hal with a pair of snowshoes, indicating they might come in handy for Hal's journey. Hal accepted the snowshoes and set out on the road. Oblivious to it all, the snow continued to fall.

At the chapel Hal stopped and looked back. Once again the

village revealed itself only in vague outlines, floating in the distance. Hal set down his suitcase, donned the snowshoes and considered the route ahead. He could see the line of depressions, now filling with new snow, that he had post-holed hours earlier.

Hal set out, following the line of depressions without stepping in them. The snowshoes made the going distinctly easier. Sometime later the hilltop where the man had left the grandfather clock came into sight. The clock was still there, casing open, but the man was nowhere to be seen. What had become of him? Had he gone off somewhere? Or had he fallen into the snow, thrashed about futilely, then frozen to death? Either way, it was time for Hal to move on—it was getting dark.

By the time Hal reached the highway where Jonas had let him off, dusk had fallen. No vehicle was to be seen. Hal was standing hopelessly, prepared for a long wait, when off in the distance a pair of headlights appeared. They belonged to a small yellow bus, its rounded snout marking it a relic. Hal huffed onto the highway with his suitcase and waved his arms. The bus sped toward Hal then slowed to a halt, engine wheezing. As luck would have it, the bus was bound for Vilnius. Hal climbed aboard.

Head resting against the frosty window, Hal gazed vacantly at the tenebrous landscape as snow-covered woods and fields passed by. The occasional town came and went, faintly visible within its cloak of darkness.

Arriving in Vilnius, Hal checked his watch, it was seven o'clock. But the ice-covered streets were empty and the night felt much later.

From the bus terminal Hal toddled along the icy streets to the Hotel Užupis. The ground-floor lounge, unlike two nights ago, was a rowdy dance hall filled with raucous music. Hal went inside, covered with snow, face ridden with fatigue. At the front desk he asked if anyone had called for him or left a message. 'No' and 'no' were the answers.

Hal went back outside and made a beeline for the Vilnius Municipal Theater. He found it with no trouble, having memorized the sketch map on the program Alvydas had given him that morning. It was seven fifty-five—his timing was perfect. Before going in Hal looked about for Alvydas. But the playwright was nowhere in sight—he must have been busy with last-minute preparations before curtain-up.

Inside, Hal saw that the building was too spacious for theatrical use. There was a balcony, but because of the small audience, it had been roped off. Some forty or fifty people were seated in the stalls, waiting for the curtain to rise.

Hal looked about for Alvydas. No, he wasn't among the audience, nor was he in the balcony. Presently the lights went down and the curtain rose to reveal a platform at a train station in the city. Awaiting the train were families with huge bundles of belongings. Hal remained ignorant of their situation, for he understood not a word of the dialogue. He could only guess that the people were being forced to move to some far land, such as Siberia. When a drunken man joined the waiting passengers and began picking quarrels with them, a portly housewife scolded him up and down, drawing scornful laughter from the others onstage. In response to the snub the boozer launched into a lengthy monologue that drew titters from the audience. Hal couldn't understand the reason for the laughter any more than he understood the actors' lines.

Enter a man with a huge suitcase. Scanning the others with a grave expression, he began a muted soliloquy that sounded like a poem being recited. The spotlight fell on him. Was this man the protagonist?

From offstage came a train whistle, followed by an announcement. Those on the platform hefted their belongings, preparing to board. Just then an elegantly dressed young woman made her appearance, panting—she was not going to miss the train. Was this the heroine? Following her with a bag was a farmer. There sounded the metallic screech of wheels coming to a stop, and the stage lights gradually dimmed.

Hal looked about the audience. All the faces were somber. He looked up toward the balcony, and there was Alvydas, all by himself, gazing at the stage, following the performance.

The stage lights came back up to reveal a train compartment

seen head on. All the passengers from the previous scene were settled in their seats, and all the faces were gloomy. At the very front of the compartment sat the man with the huge suitcase, facing the audience as he read a book. Standing in the aisle was the boozer, drinking from a bottle of vodka as he delivered a long monologue. The speech was met with an occasional chortle from the audience. Hal looked back toward the balcony. Alvydas was still there, resting his chin on the railing, gazing intently at the stage.

The heroine came down the aisle. When she saw the protagonist, she was startled, and then with obvious delight said something to him. The protagonist, though, didn't seem to recognize her. They conversed for a short while and then behind them a man got to his feet and began playing a Lithuanian folk instrument. All the other passengers rose and watched the performer. While the musician played, the woman continued to talk to the man. Hal was suddenly overcome with drowsiness and began to nod off—jet lag was still making itself felt, as was his round-trip on the snowy roads to Adutiskis. In no time he was asleep.

In his dream he saw a snow-covered hilltop where a man stood next to a grandfather clock, staring up at a sky filled with birds. Amid the bobbing birds was the Užupis flag, fluttering in the wind. Hal lurched awake. His gaze returned to the stage. A woman was dancing in the aisle of the train compartment. The other passengers were clapping in time with the music. And people in the audience began clapping in time with the actors. Just then an angel descended from above. Landing gently on the stage, she said something to the passengers. Hal looked back up and saw Alvydas, gauging the audience's reaction. Wanting to avoid Alvydas noticing him, Hal quickly returned his eyes to the stage. The man at the front of the compartment was writing fervently in a notebook. A poem? wondered Hal. Seeing the stage lights converge upon this man, Hal thought that perhaps the dancing and the angel were a re-creation of part of the poem. Again Hal sank back into slumber.

This time Hal saw the man with the huge suitcase waiting for a bus beside a highway stretching out through a desolate expanse. How could a stage set be so realistic, like something out of a movie? He would have to ask how Alvydas had managed that. This thought brought Hal wide awake, and there on the stage were two men dressed like mounted bandits, pistols in hand, threatening the passengers on the train. But when the bandits came upon the protagonist, they were visibly startled, and they adopted a posture of obvious respect. Once again Hal dropped off.

A sigh from someone nearby jolted Hal awake. He had no idea how much time had passed. On stage, the man with the huge suitcase was waiting for a bus. The backdrop showed a highway stretching out through a desolate expanse. But it was a crude job, and not very realistic. Once again Hal fell asleep.

Not long afterward Hal was awakened by clapping. The curtain had fallen and the house lights were coming up. Was Alvydas still there? Quickly he looked back. Yes, he was still up in the balcony, all by himself. Relieved, Hal turned back and joined in the applause. The curtain rose again and the players came out in turn for a bow. With each bow the applause rose to a crescendo. Hal rose and climbed up to the balcony with his suitcase.

"Hey, Hal!" cried Alvydas in delight.

Hal took Alvydas's extended hand. "You're a genius!"

"Not really," said Alvydas, managing to suppress his pleasure. "Could you understand the story?"

"Not the details, of course—I couldn't catch a word of the dialogue—but the general outline I think I figured out, I guess because it's structured so perfectly. And the performances were perfect too—in terms of pathos I couldn't ask for anything more. In particular I was struck by the protagonist."

Alvydas nodded in complete agreement. "That is Aleksandr—he was named best actor at the St. Petersburg Drama Festival." He punctuated this statement with another nod.

"But if the play isn't good, then even the best actor can't display his talents to the full," said Hal.

Alvydas nodded again. "Was any part of the play not to your liking?"

Hal paused, then phrased his answer with care: "It seemed almost perfect to me. But there's one thing…"

Alvydas listened, alert.

"One thing," Hal repeated. "These days, whether it's a play or a movie, directors don't use the inside view enough."

"What do you mean?" said Alvydas, intensely curious.

"Take the scene on the train, when the people are dancing and the angel comes down, but the spotlight is on the protagonist writing poetry—the audience sees what he's writing. They actually see what's going on inside a character. That's what I mean by the inside view. In this sense, the soliloquy, which playwrights have always used to keep their story moving along, is also a kind of inside view."

Alvydas was thrilled—everything had suddenly become clear to him. "Say, that is a really interesting point. I never thought of it like that."

"But I don't mean this as a criticism of your play. I think the reason playwrights don't use the inside view more often is that it can give away the whole story instead of allowing the audience to figure it out."

"You are right!" said Alvydas. "It makes perfect sense."

"On the other hand," said Hal, "if you get rid of the inside view, then you're left with a play that depends only on the outside view, and that doesn't always work—that's why in contemporary plays the story line tends to be killed off."

Alvydas nodded vigorously.

Down below, the audience had begun to slip out of the theater. Hal looked down at the empty seats. "How is Vilma doing?"

"I think she is going to be all right. It looks like she will leave the hospital tomorrow. But she will have to rest up at home for a while."

"That's good," Hal said, heaving a sigh of relief.

"You should not blame yourself for what happened," said Alvydas. "And Inga feels exactly the same. She told me she saw you last night."

"I'm pleased you understand," Hal said. And then, hesitantly, "Would I be able to see Miss Vilma?"

Alvydas considered this before replying. "Why do you want to see her?"

"Well... even if it's no fault of mine what happened to her ... it's clear to me that I bear some sort of moral responsibility."

"Moral responsibility? Maybe the fact that we exist in this world means we should all have some kind of moral responsibility for others." Alvydas produced a hollow chuckle. "So, how do you propose to fulfill your moral responsibility? Meet with Vilma and try to cheer her up? That sounds pretty tedious to me."

"I guess you're right," Hal said, deflated. "Even if I saw her, there wouldn't be anything I could do to help."

Hal noticed the stage crew and the actors looking for Alvydas. It was time to say goodbye. As they shook hands Alvydas suggested that they meet again.

"If we can," said Hal with a wan smile.

Outside the snow was falling fast and hard. Visibility was limited. Some of the playgoers were clearing snow from the windshields of their cars, others couldn't get their cars going and were pushing them along, hoping to start them up by popping the clutch.

Hal gazed at the streets buried in snow, and jolted into action, a man with a purpose. After a short interval of wandering, he found his bearings and made his way to Café Mano.

Inside, Hal went to the bar and asked the tall, blond-haired young man if Zoja had gone home for the day. Yes, said the young man. Hal ordered a shot of *pálinka* and asked for writing paper. The young man reached beneath the bar and came up with a dozen sheets, asking Hal to return whatever was left over. Thanking the young man, Hal took a seat at the table he and Rimas had occupied, and began to write:

My dear friend Rimas,

Almost two days have passed, and from the looks of things—my messages for you not picked up, no messages from you to me— you must have gotten yourself on that bus for Kishinev yesterday morning. And if that's the case, that bus is probably going through a dark, snow-covered forest about now—you told me it takes three days to get to Kishinev by way of Warsaw.

Here in Vilnius it's been snowing heavily. I just wish this snowstorm had started two days ago. Then you wouldn't have been able to leave, and I wouldn't be writing this letter. But that's just me being selfish.

If my hunch is right and you're on that bus to Kishinev, then it may be that you'll never read this letter. Unless you happen to return to Vilnius around this time next year and by some sheer coincidence are delivered this letter—but the chances of that are slim. Even so, there is a reason why I'm writing a letter that you may very well never read, and it is this: in my judgment there are two things I must tell you.

First, I pray with all my heart that your brother in Moldova makes a full recovery. I know you told me it's too late for him, but what I want to tell you is not to jump to conclusions. Twenty years ago someone I know was diagnosed with a brain tumor, and he is still alive and well. The tumor hasn't grown in all that time. And this is not an isolated case. I read a report somewhere that cancerous cells, for whatever reason, sometimes stop growing and metastasizing. So in my opinion you absolutely shouldn't give up hope. I'd be grateful if you could pass on my views to Donata and your nephews.

Second, this morning I heard some sad news from Alvydas, a gifted playwright and producer from Lithuania. It's about Miss Vilma, and I feel duty-bound to report it to you—it's been weighing me down all day. According to Alvydas, Miss Vilma attempted suicide last night. (Don't be alarmed, I beg of you. Alvydas just now reassured me that she is much better and could be released from the hospital as early as tomorrow.) Needless to say, I have no idea why Miss Vilma did something so reckless. I say this because I haven't yet been able to visit her. Of course, I think it's my duty to visit her, for the sake of my friendship with you, if nothing else. Alvydas, though, sees it differently: my visit to her wouldn't be helpful, and in fact it might be harmful. He was adamant about this. And what he says makes sense: at this point it's absolutely essential that Miss Vilma is stabilized psychologically. Which is why I haven't visited her.

> I think that at first Alvydas believed I had something to do with Miss Vilma's desperation. He thought she had a terrible shock when I went to the Ministry of Foreign Affairs and obtained a marriage license, but then didn't marry her. But now Alvydas realizes he was mistaken—as does Vilma's sister, Inga. And I hope that you will not misunderstand either.

The blond-haired young man arrived with Hal's *pálinka*. Hal gulped it down, then took a look outside. The snow was falling as thick as ever, and the brick wall that had lost its cement could not be seen. Hal returned to his letter. A good hour later his pen came to a stop and Hal read over what he had written, jotted down the date and the time, and finally signed it. Folding the letter and sticking it into his coat pocket, he rose.

Hal's next stop was the hotel. At the front desk he asked if there had been any callers, or any messages left. None, came the answer. Could he have the envelope he had left there that morning? Hal asked. By all means, said the clerk, retrieving it for him. To the message and letter Hal had written earlier he added the letter he had just written at Café Mano. Re-sealing the now thick envelope, he wrote "To my friend Rimas" on the outside and handed it to the clerk.

"If anyone comes looking for me, could you give him this?"

"By all means," said the clerk, putting it away.

"Well, so long," said Hal.

"Good luck," said the clerk.

Back outside, visibility had deteriorated to less than a foot. Hal set out but immediately lost his way. He roamed for some time, and suddenly, there in front of him was the Vilnia River. The hour was late, and he had seen no one else out and about. He looked in all directions, trying to guess exactly where he was in the city. But so much snow was falling he could make out nothing.

Just then he glimpsed a figure coming toward him out of the gloom. Hal was elated and at the same time terrified. Coughing loudly to signal his presence, he called out, "Who's there?"

But the person made no reply; there was only the echo of

Hal's voice, returning to him from the snow-buried city.

"I've lost my way!" Hal shouted. "Where am I?"

Again he heard only the echo of his own voice; there was no response from his counterpart. Hal felt for the revolver in his pocket, his index finger curling around the trigger.

Finally the figure began to take shape. Faintly illuminated by a streetlight was a towering man. Fortunately for Hal, the man didn't look violent. His cheeks were hollow and his shoulders drooped lifelessly. He looked like a discouraged job seeker—had he just returned from a long exile in Siberia?

Noticing how fatigued and lifeless the man looked, Hal thought better of trying to talk to him. Feeling empathy along with trepidation he made way for the man.

The man walked past him, and then from the darkness Hal heard a voice: "Hal, is that you?"

A shiver ran through him. The words were neither Lithuanian nor English—they were Užupis. Hal could see the man had turned back toward him.

"Was that you?" Hal shouted toward the man. But the words coming out of his mouth were English, not Užupis. Hal tried again, this time in Užupis, but the words wouldn't come.

From out of the darkness came the same voice: "Hal—is that you? You've come back, haven't you?"

Because the man was standing stock still, Hal couldn't be certain it was he who had spoken. Hal called out again: "How do you know me?" Again in English. Poor Hal, he had lost the ability to speak Užupis, though he still understood it.

"My name is Urbonas," came the voice from the darkness. "I knew you'd come back."

"Urbonas!" Hal shouted, shuddering in ecstasy and surprise.

Just then, from out of an alley came a police cruiser, lights flashing. The man took one look and ran off.

"Wait!" Hal shouted. "Wait just a minute!"

But the man had been swallowed up in the darkness.

For the next hour Hal drifted through dim night calling for Urbonas. Finally he came to the mouth of an alley. In the faint illumination of a streetlight he found the message from Jurgita, given to him by the farmer with the goose. He considered a moment, then set off again and soon reached the courtyard to Jurgita's apartment building.

Crossing the white carpet of snow, he entered the building and climbed the lighted stairway to the fourth floor. At Jurgita's door he removed his cap and shook the snow from it. He did likewise with his coat. And finally he stamped his feet on the mat. He pressed the doorbell. No answer. He pressed it again, this time longer. Again no answer. Remembering Jurgita's routine, he found the loose brick, removed it, and stuck a hand inside. The key to her apartment was cold to his fingers.

He opened the door and was greeted by stillness. Before entering he cleaned the soles of his shoes on the rug. Then he felt along the wall, found the switch, and turned on the light.

Nothing was there; the apartment was vacant. He took in the living room, but saw only a frayed couch and a small table. The flag was gone from the wall, and the photos that had been on the mantelpiece were nowhere to be seen.

Hal checked the bedroom where he had spent the previous night with Jurgita. There was only the wood floor, layered with dust. It looked like no one had lived here for some time. Hal nodded once, then nodded again. Somehow he wasn't surprised. He returned to the living room and placed his hat and coat on the back of the couch. And there he sat.

He pondered a brief while, then rose and went to his suitcase. From it he took each of the items he had been carrying all this time. The funeral urn wrapped in black cloth he set on the table, along with the funeral portrait of his father. And on top of the urn he placed the red rose he had bought from Marija last night.

From his pocket he took the revolver. From another pocket he took the cartridge case. From the case he took a handful of bullets and with no wasted motion loaded the revolver with six of them. Back into the case went the remaining bullets. He spun the cylinder once, as if playing Russian roulette, placed the muzzle against his temple, and pulled the trigger. There was a sharp crack and Hal was sent sprawling onto the floor. He died mouth half open, eyes gazing into space, as if they had found his long-sought fatherland.

The next morning snow was still falling onto the courtyard of Jurgita's apartment building. The police loaded a stretcher into a waiting ambulance with flashing lights. On the stretcher lay the body of an unidentified Asian man.

There followed the short Lithuanian spring and the equally short summer and autumn, and then the long winter returned. One day Jurgita took the items from Hal's suitcase and arranged them in her display cabinets. As she was finishing this task she heard the cry of her baby awakening. She rushed to the crib, took the crying baby in her arms, and sat on the frayed couch, the last place Hal had been. Unbuttoning her blouse she unveiled a breast, so fair and full and lovely, and put it to the baby's mouth. Eagerly the baby began to suck.

The solemn and sorrowful strains of the Užupis national anthem filled the room. Outside it continued to snow.

As she suckled the baby Jurgita murmured, "Gerdihal. Oh, my little Gerdihal." Tears streamed from her huge, limpid eyes.

LIBRARY OF KOREAN LITERATURE
DALKEY ARCHIVE PRESS

1. *STINGRAY*
KIM JOO-YOUNG

2. *ONE SPOON ON THIS EARTH*
HYUN KI YOUNG

3. *WHEN ADAM OPENS HIS EYES*
JANG JUNG-IL

4. *MY SON'S GIRLFRIEND*
JUNG MI-KYUNG

5. *A MOST AMBIGUOUS SUNDAY, AND OTHER STORIES*
JUNG YOUNG MOON

6. *THE HOUSE WITH A SUNKEN COURTYARD*
KIM WON-IL

7. *AT LEAST WE CAN APOLOGIZE*
LEE KI-HO

8. *THE SOIL*
YI KWANG-SU

9. *LONESOME YOU*
PARK WAN-SUH

10. *NO ONE WRITES BACK*
JANG EUN-JIN

11. *PAVANE FOR A DEAD PRINCESS*
PARK MIN-GYU

12. *THE SQUARE*
CHOI IN-HUN

13. *SCENES FROM THE ENLIGHTENMENT: A NOVEL OF MANNERS*
KIM NAMCHEON

14. *ANOTHER MAN'S CITY*
CH'OE IN-HO

15. *THE REPUBLIC OF UŽUPIS*
HAÏLJI

SELECTED DALKEY ARCHIVE TITLES

MICHAL AJVAZ, *The Golden Age*.
The Other City.
PIERRE ALBERT-BIROT, *Grabinoulor*.
YUZ ALESHKOVSKY, *Kangaroo*.
FELIPE ALFAU, *Chromos*. *Locos*.
IVAN ÂNGELO, *The Celebration*.
The Tower of Glass.
ANTÓNIO LOBO ANTUNES, *Knowledge of Hell*.
The Splendor of Portugal.
ALAIN ARIAS-MISSON, *Theatre of Incest*.
JOHN ASHBERY & JAMES SCHUYLER, *A Nest of Ninnies*.
ROBERT ASHLEY, *Perfect Lives*.
GABRIELA AVIGUR-ROTEM, *Heatwave and Crazy Birds*.
DJUNA BARNES, *Ladies Almanack*.
Ryder.
JOHN BARTH, *Letters*. *Sabbatical*.
DONALD BARTHELME, *The King*.
Paradise.
SVETISLAV BASARA, *Chinese Letter*.
MIQUEL BAUÇÀ, *The Siege in the Room*.
RENÉ BELLETTO, *Dying*.
MAREK BIENCZYK, *Transparency*.
ANDREI BITOV, *Pushkin House*.
ANDREJ BLATNIK, *You Do Understand*.
LOUIS PAUL BOON, *Chapel Road*.
My Little War.
Summer in Termuren.
ROGER BOYLAN, *Killoyle*.
IGNÁCIO DE LOYOLA BRANDÃO, *Zero*.
Anonymous Celebrity.
BONNIE BREMSER, *Troia: Mexican Memoirs*.
CHRISTINE BROOKE-ROSE, *Amalgamemnon*.
BRIGID BROPHY, *In Transit*.
GERALD L. BRUNS, *Modern Poetry and the Idea of Language*.
GABRIELLE BURTON, *Heartbreak Hotel*.
MICHEL BUTOR, *Degrees*. *Mobile*.

G. CABRERA INFANTE, *Infante's Inferno*.
Three Trapped Tigers.
ARNO CAMENISCH, *The Alp*.
JULIETA CAMPOS, *The Fear of Losing Eurydice*.
ANNE CARSON, *Eros the Bittersweet*.
ORLY CASTEL-BLOOM, *Dolly City*.
LOUIS-FERDINAND CÉLINE, *North*.
Rigadoon.
Castle to Castle.
Conversations with Professor Y.
London Bridge.
Normance.
MARIE CHAIX, *The Laurels of Lake Constance*.
HUGO CHARTERIS, *The Tide Is Right*.
ERIC CHEVILLARD, *Demolishing Nisard*.
MARC CHOLODENKO, *Mordechai Schamz*.
JOSHUA COHEN, *Witz*.
EMILY HOLMES COLEMAN, *The Shutter of Snow*.
ROBERT COOVER, *A Night at the Movies*.
STANLEY CRAWFORD, *Log of the S.S. The Mrs Unguentine*.
Some Instructions to My Wife.
S.D. CHROSTOWSKA, *Permission*.
RENÉ CREVEL, *Putting My Foot in It*.
RALPH CUSACK, *Cadenza*.
NICHOLAS DELBANCO, *Sherbrookes*.
The Count of Concord.
NIGEL DENNIS, *Cards of Identity*.
PETER DIMOCK, *A Short Rhetoric for Leaving the Family*.
ARIEL DORFMAN, *Konfidenz*.
COLEMAN DOWELL, *Island People*.
Too Much Flesh and Jabez.
ARKADII DRAGOMOSHCHENKO, *Dust*.
RIKKI DUCORNET, *Phosphor in Dreamland*.
The Complete Butcher's Tales.
The Jade Cabinet.
The Fountains of Neptune.

FOR A FULL LIST OF PUBLICATIONS, VISIT: www.dalkeyarchive.com

SELECTED DALKEY ARCHIVE TITLES

WILLIAM EASTLAKE, *The Bamboo Bed.*
Castle Keep.
Lyric of the Circle Heart.
JEAN ECHENOZ, *Chopin's Move.*
STANLEY ELKIN, *A Bad Man.*
Criers and Kibitzers, Kibitzers and Criers.
The Dick Gibson Show.
The Franchiser.
The Living End.
Mrs. Ted Bliss.
FRANÇOIS EMMANUEL, *Invitation to a Voyage.*
SALVADOR ESPRIU, *Ariadne in the Grotesque Labyrinth.*
LESLIE A. FIEDLER, *Love and Death in the American Novel.*
JUAN FILLOY, *Op Oloop.*
ANDY FITCH, *Pop Poetics.*
GUSTAVE FLAUBERT, *Bouvard and Pécuchet.*
KASS FLEISHER, *Talking out of School.*
JON FOSSE, *Aliss at the Fire.*
Melancholy.
FORD MADOX FORD, *The March of Literature.*
MAX FRISCH, *I'm Not Stiller.*
Man in the Holocene.
CARLOS FUENTES, *Adam in Eden.*
Christopher Unborn.
Distant Relations.
Terra Nostra.
Where the Air Is Clear.
TAKEHIKO FUKUNAGA, *Flowers of Grass.*
WILLIAM GADDIS, JR., *The Recognitions.*
JANICE GALLOWAY, *Foreign Parts.*
The Trick Is to Keep Breathing.
WILLIAM H. GASS, *Cartesian Sonata and Other Novellas.*
The Tunnel.
Willie Masters' Lonesome Wife.
GÉRARD GAVARRY, *Hoppla! 1 2 3.*
ETIENNE GILSON, *The Arts of the Beautiful.*
Forms and Substances in the Arts.

C. S. GISCOMBE, *Giscome Road.*
Here.
DOUGLAS GLOVER, *Bad News of the Heart.*
WITOLD GOMBROWICZ, *A Kind of Testament.*
PAULO EMÍLIO SALES GOMES, *P's Three Women.*
GEORGI GOSPODINOV, *Natural Novel.*
JUAN GOYTISOLO, *Count Julian.*
Juan the Landless.
Makbara.
Marks of Identity.
HENRY GREEN, *Back.*
Blindness.
Concluding.
Doting.
Nothing.
JACK GREEN, *Fire the Bastards!*
JIŘÍ GRUŠA, *The Questionnaire.*
MELA HARTWIG, *Am I a Redundant Human Being?*
JOHN HAWKES, *The Passion Artist.*
Whistlejacket.
ELIZABETH HEIGHWAY, ED., *Contemporary Georgian Fiction.*
ALEKSANDAR HEMON, ED., *Best European Fiction.*
AIDAN HIGGINS, *Balcony of Europe.*
Blind Man's Bluff.
Bornholm Night-Ferry.
Flotsam and Jetsam.
Langrishe, Go Down.
Scenes from a Receding Past.
KEIZO HINO, *Isle of Dreams.*
KAZUSHI HOSAKA, *Plainsong.*
ALDOUS HUXLEY, *Antic Hay.*
Crome Yellow.
Point Counter Point.
Those Barren Leaves.
Time Must Have a Stop.
NAOYUKI II, *The Shadow of a Blue Cat.*
GERT JONKE, *Awakening to the Great Sleep War.*
The Distant Sound.

FOR A FULL LIST OF PUBLICATIONS, VISIT: www.dalkeyarchive.com

SELECTED DALKEY ARCHIVE TITLES

GERT JONKE (cont.), *Geometric Regional Novel.*
Homage to Czerny.
The System of Vienna.
JACQUES JOUET, *Mountain R. Savage.*
Upstaged.
MIEKO KANAI, *The Word Book.*
YORAM KANIUK, *Life on Sandpaper.*
HUGH KENNER, *Flaubert.*
Joyce and Beckett: The Stoic Comedians.
Joyce's Voices.
DANILO KIŠ, *The Attic.*
Garden, Ashes.
The Lute and the Scars.
Psalm 44.
A Tomb for Boris Davidovich.
ANITA KONKKA, *A Fool's Paradise.*
GEORGE KONRÁD, *The City Builder.*
TADEUSZ KONWICKI, *A Minor Apocalypse.*
The Polish Complex.
MENIS KOUMANDAREAS, *Koula.*
ELAINE KRAF, *The Princess of 72nd Street.*
JIM KRUSOE, *Iceland.*
AYSE KULIN, *Farewell: A Mansion in Occupied Istanbul.*
EMILIO LASCANO TEGUI, *On Elegance While Sleeping.*
ERIC LAURRENT, *Do Not Touch.*
VIOLETTE LEDUC, *La Bâtarde.*
EDOUARD LEVÉ, *Autoportrait.*
Suicide.
Works.
MARIO LEVI, *Istanbul Was a Fairy Tale.*
DEBORAH LEVY, *Billy and Girl.*
JOSÉ LEZAMA LIMA, *Paradiso.*
ROSA LIKSOM, *Dark Paradise.*
OSMAN LINS, *Avalovara.*
The Queen of the Prisons of Greece.
ALF MAC LOCHLAINN, *Out of Focus.*
The Corpus in the Library.
RON LOEWINSOHN, *Magnetic Field(s).*
MINA LOY, *Stories and Essays of Mina Loy.*
J.M. MACHADO DE ASSIS, *Stories.*

MELISSA MALOUF, *More Than You Know.*
D. KEITH MANO, *Take Five.*
MICHELINE AHARONIAN MARCOM, *The Mirror in the Well.*
A Brief History of Yes.
BEN MARCUS, *The Age of Wire and String.*
WALLACE MARKFIELD, *Teitlebaum's Window.*
To an Early Grave.
DAVID MARKSON, *Reader's Block.*
Wittgenstein's Mistress.
CAROLE MASO, *AVA.*
LADISLAV MATEJKA & KRYSTYNA POMORSKA, EDS., *Readings in Russian Poetics: Formalist and Structuralist Views.*
HARRY MATHEWS, *Cigarettes.*
The Conversions.
The Human Country: New and Collected Stories.
The Journalist.
My Life in CIA.
Singular Pleasures.
The Sinking of the Odradek.
Stadium.
Tlooth.
JOSEPH MCELROY, *Night Soul and Other Stories.*
DONAL MCLAUGHLIN, *beheading the virgin mary.*
ABDELWAHAB MEDDEB, *Talismano.*
GERHARD MEIER, *Isle of the Dead.*
HERMAN MELVILLE, *The Confidence-Man.*
AMANDA MICHALOPOULOU, *I'd Like.*
STEVEN MILLHAUSER, *The Barnum Museum.*
In the Penny Arcade.
RALPH J. MILLS, JR., *Essays on Poetry.*
MOMUS, *The Book of Jokes.*
CHRISTINE MONTALBETTI, *The Origin of Man.*
Western.
OLIVE MOORE, *Spleen.*

FOR A FULL LIST OF PUBLICATIONS, VISIT: www.dalkeyarchive.com

SELECTED DALKEY ARCHIVE TITLES

NICHOLAS MOSLEY, *Accident.*
Assassins.
Catastrophe Practice.
Experience and Religion.
A Garden of Trees.
Hopeful Monsters.
Imago Bird.
Impossible Object.
Inventing God.
Judith.
Look at the Dark.
Natalie Natalia.
Serpent.
Time at War.
WARREN MOTTE, *Fables of the Novel: French Fiction since 1990.*
Fiction Now: The French Novel in the 21st Century.
Oulipo: A Primer of Potential Literature.
GERALD MURNANE, *Barley Patch.*
Inland.
YVES NAVARRE, *Our Share of Time.*
Sweet Tooth.
DOROTHY NELSON, *In Night's City.*
Tar and Feathers.
ESHKOL NEVO, *Homesick.*
WILFRIDO D. NOLLEDO, *But for the Lovers.*
FLANN O'BRIEN, *At Swim-Two-Birds.*
The Best of Myles.
The Dalkey Archive.
The Hard Life.
The Poor Mouth.
The Third Policeman.
CLAUDE OLLIER, *The Mise-en-Scène.*
Wert and the Life Without End.
GIOVANNI ORELLI, *Walaschek's Dream.*
PATRIK OUŘEDNÍK, *Europeana.*
The Opportune Moment, 1855.
BORIS PAHOR, *Necropolis.*
FERNANDO DEL PASO, *News from the Empire.*
Palinuro of Mexico.
ROBERT PINGET, *The Inquisitory.*
Mahu or The Material.
Trio.

MANUEL PUIG, *Betrayed by Rita Hayworth.*
The Buenos Aires Affair.
Heartbreak Tango.
RAYMOND QUENEAU, *The Last Days.*
Odile.
Pierrot Mon Ami.
Saint Glinglin.
ANN QUIN, *Berg.*
Passages.
Three.
Tripticks.
ISHMAEL REED, *The Free-Lance Pallbearers.*
The Last Days of Louisiana Red.
Ishmael Reed: The Plays.
Juice!
Reckless Eyeballing.
The Terrible Threes.
The Terrible Twos.
Yellow Back Radio Broke-Down.
JASIA REICHARDT, *15 Journeys Warsaw to London.*
NOËLLE REVAZ, *With the Animals.*
JOÃO UBALDO RIBEIRO, *House of the Fortunate Buddhas.*
JEAN RICARDOU, *Place Names.*
RAINER MARIA RILKE, *The Notebooks of Malte Laurids Brigge.*
JULIÁN RÍOS, *The House of Ulysses.*
Larva: A Midsummer Night's Babel.
Poundemonium.
Procession of Shadows.
AUGUSTO ROA BASTOS, *I the Supreme.*
DANIËL ROBBERECHTS, *Arriving in Avignon.*
JEAN ROLIN, *The Explosion of the Radiator Hose.*
OLIVIER ROLIN, *Hotel Crystal.*
ALIX CLEO ROUBAUD, *Alix's Journal.*
JACQUES ROUBAUD, *The Form of a City Changes Faster, Alas, Than the Human Heart.*
The Great Fire of London.
Hortense in Exile.
Hortense is Abducted.

FOR A FULL LIST OF PUBLICATIONS, VISIT: www.dalkeyarchive.com

SELECTED DALKEY ARCHIVE TITLES

JACQUES ROUBAUD (cont.), *The Loop.*
  Mathematics: The Plurality of Worlds of Lewis.
  The Princess Hoppy.
  Some Thing Black.
RAYMOND ROUSSEL, *Impressions of Africa.*
VEDRANA RUDAN, *Night.*
STIG SÆTERBAKKEN, *Siamese.*
  Self Control.
  Through the Night.
LYDIE SALVAYRE, *The Company of Ghosts.*
  The Lecture.
  The Power of Flies.
LUIS RAFAEL SÁNCHEZ, *Macho Camacho's Beat.*
SEVERO SARDUY, *Cobra & Maitreya.*
NATHALIE SARRAUTE, *Do You Hear Them?*
  Martereau.
  The Planetarium.
ARNO SCHMIDT, *Collected Novellas.*
  Collected Stories.
  Nobodaddy's Children.
  Two Novels.
ASAF SCHURR, *Motti.*
GAIL SCOTT, *My Paris.*
DAMION SEARLS, *What We Were Doing and Where We Were Going.*
JUNE AKERS SEESE, *Is This What Other Women Feel Too?*
  What Waiting Really Means.
BERNARD SHARE, *Inish. Transit.*
VIKTOR SHKLOVSKY, *Bowstring.*
  Knight's Move.
  A Sentimental Journey: Memoirs 1917–1922.
  Energy of Delusion: A Book on Plot.
  Literature and Cinematography.
  Theory of Prose.
  Third Factory.
  Zoo, or Letters Not about Love.
PIERRE SINIAC, *The Collaborators.*
KJERSTI A. SKOMSVOLD, *The Faster I Walk, the Smaller I Am.*

JOSEF ŠKVORECKÝ, *The Engineer of Human Souls.*
GILBERT SORRENTINO, *Aberration of Starlight.*
  Blue Pastoral.
  Crystal Vision.
  Imaginative Qualities of Actual Things.
  Mulligan Stew.
  Pack of Lies.
  Red the Fiend.
  The Sky Changes.
  Something Said.
  Splendide-Hôtel.
  Steelwork.
  Under the Shadow.
W. M. SPACKMAN, *The Complete Fiction.*
ANDRZEJ STASIUK, *Dukla.*
  Fado.
GERTRUDE STEIN, *The Making of Americans.*
  A Novel of Thank You.
GWEN LI SUI (ED.), *Telltale: 11 Stories.*
LARS SVENDSEN, *A Philosophy of Evil.*
PIOTR SZEWC, *Annihilation.*
GONÇALO M. TAVARES, *Jerusalem.*
  Joseph Walser's Machine.
  Learning to Pray in the Age of Technique.
LUCIAN DAN TEODOROVICI, *Our Circus Presents…*
NIKANOR TERATOLOGEN, *Assisted Living.*
STEFAN THEMERSON, *Hobson's Island.*
  The Mystery of the Sardine.
  Tom Harris.
TAEKO TOMIOKA, *Building Waves.*
JOHN TOOMEY, *Sleepwalker.*
JEAN-PHILIPPE TOUSSAINT,
  The Bathroom.
  Camera.
  Monsieur.
  Reticence.
  Running Away.
  Self-Portrait Abroad.
  Television.
  The Truth about Marie.

FOR A FULL LIST OF PUBLICATIONS, VISIT: www.dalkeyarchive.com

SELECTED DALKEY ARCHIVE TITLES

DUMITRU TSEPENEAG, *Hotel Europa.*
The Necessary Marriage.
Pigeon Post.
Vain Art of the Fugue.
ESTHER TUSQUETS, *Stranded.*
DUBRAVKA UGRESIC, *Lend Me Your Character.*
Thank You for Not Reading.
TOR ULVEN, *Replacement.*
MATI UNT, *Brecht at Night.*
Diary of a Blood Donor.
Things in the Night.
ÁLVARO URIBE & OLIVIA SEARS, EDS., *Best of Contemporary Mexican Fiction.*
ELOY URROZ, *Friction.*
The Obstacles.
BUKET UZUNER, *I am Istanbul.*
LUISA VALENZUELA, *Dark Desires and the Others.*
He Who Searches.
PAUL VERHAEGHEN, *Omega Minor.*
AGLAJA VETERANYI, *Why the Child is Cooking in the Polenta.*
BORIS VIAN, *Heartsnatcher.*
LLORENÇ VILLALONGA, *The Dolls' Room.*
TOOMAS VINT, *An Unending Landscape.*
IGOR VISHNEVETSKY, *Leningrad.*
ORNELA VORPSI, *The Country Where No One Ever Dies.*
AUSTRYN WAINHOUSE, *Hedyphagetica.*
CURTIS WHITE, *America's Magic Mountain.*
The Idea of Home.
Memories of My Father Watching TV.
Requiem.
DIANE WILLIAMS, *Excitability: Selected Stories.*
Romancer Erector.
DOUGLAS WOOLF, *Wall to Wall.*
Ya! & John-Juan.
JAY WRIGHT, *Polynomials and Pollen.*
The Presentable Art of Reading Absence.
PHILIP WYLIE, *Generation of Vipers.*

MARGUERITE YOUNG, *Angel in the Forest.*
Miss MacIntosh, My Darling.
REYOUNG, *Unbabbling.*
VLADO ŽABOT, *The Succubus.*
ZORAN ŽIVKOVIĆ, *Hidden Camera.*
LOUIS ZUKOFSKY, *Collected Fiction.*
VITOMIL ZUPAN, *Minuet for Guitar.*
SCOTT ZWIREN, *God Head.*

FOR A FULL LIST OF PUBLICATIONS, VISIT: www.dalkeyarchive.com